A Show of Violence

Sir Nicholas Harding, Q.C. said: 'You've told me nothing about the case so far, except that your client is a thirteen-year-old boy who killed an old man with whom he has apparently been living.'

Antony Maitland, Q.C.: 'That's really all I know myself.'

'The boy's name, at least.'

'Tommy.'

'Is that all?'

'All anyone has been able to get out of him apparently. And that he didn't do it. I don't know yet whether that is more than a routine denial.'

The case took Maitland back to the northern town of Arkenshaw where he had previously defended two very difficult cases.

Though in some ways simpler than its predecessors this one is even odder. No-one knew who the boy was, and if he knew himself he wasn't saying. It was strange to meet such obduracy in one so young who, though probably guilty, appeared neither stupid nor brutal. While the boy refused to speak there was no possible line of defence.

How Antony Maitland resolves this immovable situation is the subject of the novel. Maitland has never been more sympathetic, sensitive and perceptive than he is here. We are offered a *bona fide* classical whodunnit with clues to solve it—and a landscape familiar to the thousands of addicts of Sara Woods, who has recently provided so much excitement in *Enter the Corpse* and *Done to Death*.

A SHOW OF VIOLENCE

SARA WOODS

We do it wrong, being so majestical
To offer it the show of violence;

HAMLET, Act I, Scene i

M

© Sara Woods 1975

SBN: 333 17980 3

First published 1975 by
MACMILLAN LONDON LIMITED
London and Basingstoke
Associated companies in New York
Dublin Melbourne Johannesburg and Delhi

Printed in Great Britain by
NORTHUMBERLAND PRESS LIMITED
Gateshead

Any work of fiction whose characters were of uniform
excellence would rightly be condemned—by that fact if by
no other—as being incredibly dull. Therefore no excuse
can be considered necessary for the villainy or folly of the
people appearing in this book. It seems extremely unlikely
that any one of them should resemble a real person, alive
or dead. Any such resemblance is completely unintentional
and without malice.

S.W.

'It is becoming a habit,' said Sir Nicholas Harding austerely, 'and should not be encouraged.' He was looking at his nephew as he spoke, and Antony Maitland exchanged a helpless glance with his wife.

'You can't blame us for that, Uncle Nick,' Jenny pointed out reasonably, which proved to be a mistake.

'Blame you! It is not a question of blame,' said Sir Nicholas, and proceeded to contradict himself. 'If you had not encouraged Conway in the past, he would not now be in the habit of sending for you every time anything goes wrong.'

'It isn't a personal matter this time,' said Antony.

'I am well aware of the fact.'

'Well, I mean, it's only a brief, after all. No question of involving Jenny. That's what you're making a fuss about, isn't it?' he added unguardedly.

'Making a fuss is hardly how I should have described my sense of outrage,' said Sir Nicholas awfully, 'which I am endeavouring to convey to you in as restrained a manner as possible.'

'There's nothing to be outraged about.' A hint of doggedness had crept into Antony's tone. It was Tuesday evening, when Sir Nicholas traditionally dined with them, and he had sacrificed what remained of his best brandy in the interests of peace before he brought up the subject of Chris Conway's request, but it didn't seem to have had the desired effect. As he ought to have expected, his uncle pounced on the statement with an air of triumph.

'On the contrary,' he said, 'there is every precedent. You have been to Arkenshaw twice before—'

'Two difficult cases,' Antony pointed out, not very hopefully.

'There is nothing to say that this will not prove to be "difficult" too.'

'Oh, I don't think ... a thirteen-year-old boy. How can there be anything in it but a straight defence?'

'If that was all that was involved, Conway would surely have called on someone on the North Eastern circuit. The fact that he has asked you to undertake this tiresome journey—'

'Two and a half hours by train.'

'—is sufficient evidence that the case is not quite straightforward,' said Sir Nicholas, with the air of one producing an unanswerable argument.

'I thought you liked Chris,' Jenny put in.

'That has nothing to do with the case.'

'Well, I think it has.' Jenny had already put up her own argument against her husband accepting a brief that would take him to the north of England, but nobody, thought Antony, regarding her affectionately, would have guessed it from her manner now. She was sitting in her favourite corner of the sofa, opposite the fireplace, and the lamp that stood a little behind her shoulder gilded her brown curls but left her face in shadow. But he knew her expression so well, a kind of serenity of which even his more outrageous escapades over the years had been unable altogether to deprive her, and a gentle steadfastness that was just as much a part of her character. Now she sounded completely in earnest, though she ought to know if anyone did that it was useless to argue with Uncle Nick when he was in one of his difficult moods. 'If you like a person,' she was saying now, 'you try to help them, don't you? But anyway, Antony can't go refusing briefs right and left.

6

What would Mr Mallory say?' (Mallory was Sir Nicholas's clerk, and Sir Nicholas was the head of chambers to which his nephew also belonged.)

'What, indeed?' echoed Antony in a sombre tone. His uncle, glancing at him suspiciously, found as he had expected that his eyes were amused.

'May I remind you,' he enquired, 'that it was no longer ago than last June—'

'That was different,' said Jenny quickly. 'That was personal, and of course we had to help Chris, hadn't we? But you wouldn't expect him to keep on involving us in his own affairs. This is just a matter of business.'

'An awkward case,' said Sir Nicholas, shifting his ground. 'You may as well admit as much as that.'

'Well, I daresay. I've never known you refuse a brief because it was awkward, Uncle Nick.' And as Antony spoke the older man underwent one of his inexplicable changes of mood.

'I should think not,' he said, quite amiably. 'But you've told me nothing about the case so far, except that your client is a thirteen-year-old who killed an old man with whom he had apparently been living.'

'That's really all I know myself.'

'The boy's name, at least.'

'Tommy.'

'Is that all?'

'All anyone has been able to get out of him, apparently. And that he didn't do it. I don't know yet whether that is more than a routine denial.'

'Then it seems I must possess my soul in patience,' said Sir Nicholas. 'Is there any more coffee, Jenny? When you are in an argumentative mood, Antony, it always makes me thirsty.' But in spite of the injustice of this remark his tone was still reasonably mellow. Perhaps, after all, the brandy had not been sacrificed in vain.

7

The railway station at Arkenshaw is not at the best of times a noticeably cheerful place. In the dusk of that October day it was as though the train had drawn into a cavern. Antony Maitland followed the porter who was carrying his suitcase down the platform, and scanned the group of people who were waiting beyond the barrier for a first sight of Chris Conway, his instructing solicitor, who was punctilious in the matter of meeting trains even though Maitland's destination was only the Midland Hotel next door. And there Chris was, not looking very different from the first time they had met five years ago; a man of medium height, in his early thirties now, with rather unruly brown hair that had probably been red when he was younger. The slightly worried look was natural to him, and didn't necessarily mean trouble. Anyway, he brightened a little when he saw Antony approaching.

The car, also as usual, was parked illegally in what should have been a stand for taxis only. Chris directed the disposal of Antony's suitcase in the boot and climbed into the driver's seat only a moment after his passenger had installed himself. 'I'm taking you home for dinner,' he said, 'if that's all right with you.'

'Much more agreeable than the bar mess,' said Maitland with satisfaction.

'And then John Bushey is coming round for an informal conference. I didn't think,' said Conway, not without malice, 'that you'd want to wait until tomorrow to see him.'

'The sooner the better,' Antony agreed equably. There

8

had been a time when his own eagerness to get on with the job had left the younger man gasping, but they were used to each other's ways by now. 'It's good that you managed to get him again.' Bushey was the member of the North Eastern Circuit who had been briefed to act as his junior.

'Essential, I thought.' Chris was waiting to edge the car out of the station yard into the stream of traffic, but when Antony glanced at him he saw that he was smiling. 'I mean, he's not likely to be surprised by anything you do.'

'Uncle Nick *said* it was that kind of a case,' said Maitland, resigned.

'What kind?'

'The kind where I might be tempted to go beyond my brief. Well, he didn't exactly say that, now that I come to think of it, but he certainly implied it.'

'He didn't want you to come?'

'Don't worry. He's equally captious every time I propose going out of town. And often when I don't,' he added, in the interests of accuracy. 'It's just a matter of what mood you catch him in.'

'I'm sorry about that,' said Chris, but he sounded preoccupied now. They had turned right out of the station into Swinegate and passed the Midland Hotel leaving behind them the four lightly-draped nymphs who guard the fountain in the centre of the square, and now he was trying to edge the car into the centre lane. 'Not much further now,' he went on, but whether he was encouraging his passenger or himself wasn't clear. 'You can say this much about Ingleton Crescent, it's pretty central.'

'You can say more for it than that, I should have thought,' said Antony, eyeing the passing scene tranquilly. From here in the heart of the town you couldn't see Comstock's Mill, that loomed over it like a benevolent ogre, at once offending the eye and satisfying the needs of a large part of the population for gainful employment, nor could

9

you see the dark hills beyond the town. Only the smoke-grimed buildings had any reality, the shop windows brightly lighted, the double-decker bus that was barring their way. And at the sight of this last Maitland sat suddenly bolt upright and said, 'Heaven and earth!' in an awed tone. Chris jumped, gripped the steering wheel more tightly, and said,

'Don't *do* that!' in a peevish tone.

'But you should have warned me. You've done away with the trams.'

'It wasn't a personal decision.' Conway had got over his fright and was amused again. 'As a matter of fact, I think it was a silly idea, because the buses take up just as much room and are smelly into the bargain.'

'That's progress for you,' Maitland sympathised. They were well into the centre lane now, which was just as well, because the traffic lights were coming up where he knew they had to turn. 'I must say, it doesn't seem like Arkenshaw without them though.'

'It's about the only change there has been.' Impossible to tell whether Chris thought that was a good thing or not. He had stopped for the red light and was a little tense, waiting for the change. Which was something else that hadn't altered, Antony thought, he must surely be the most cautious driver in creation ... even when compared with his fellow Yorkshiremen, who were noted for their prudence. Or was that a fallacy?

Fallacy or no, the light changed to green. Chris pulled forward a little, waited, accomplished the turn in safety. Number eleven was the sixth house on the left from the corner ... a terrace of substantial grey stone houses, some of which had been turned into offices now. It had a green front door, newly painted like the rest of the woodwork, which opened as the car drew up. 'Thank heaven they've left me a parking space for once,' said Chris as he pulled on the hand brake. By the time they had alighted, Star Conway was half way down the steps to meet them.

As usual, Antony was amused and a little touched at the way Chris brightened at the sight of her. Not that she wasn't good to look at. Star was small, and still as slender as she had been when he first saw her five years ago. She had a cloud of dark hair, and hazel eyes, and a warm friendliness of manner. It wasn't as good as going home to Jenny, of course, but perhaps the next thing to it.

There was plenty to talk about over dinner, and Star made good coffee, and Jenny's gift to the son and heir, now peacefully asleep in his cot upstairs, had been given the seal of approval. Maitland was feeling pleasantly relaxed when the bell rang and Star said, 'That must be Mr Bushey,' and went out into the hall. She returned a moment later with the barrister in tow, fussed gently for a moment, seeing that they each had a full cup, and then took herself off with a murmured excuse.

John Bushey was a solidly built man, a few years older than his leader, and almost completely bald. He had a calm temperament (which Chris would have said was just as well), but was not without humour. He greeted his two colleagues casually, rather as if he had seen them earlier in the day instead of, in Maitland's case, over three years ago. That done, he seated himself in the chair Star had vacated at the right of the fire and pulled out a pipe. 'If Mrs Conway won't mind,' he said, and Conway, in honour bound, replied, 'Of course not,' and Maitland thought that it was the worst thing he knew about his junior, this predilection for a singularly unfragrant tobacco. But there wasn't anything to be done about it, and at least he couldn't smoke in court.

'Well now,' said Bushey, 'what do you think of this business then?'

'I was hoping,' said Antony, choosing his words, 'that

perhaps Conway had some more information for us on which to base an opinion.'

'Just what was in your brief,' said Chris.

It was difficult to escape the conclusion that he was being deliberately tantalising. 'The bare bones,' Maitland pointed out.

'I suppose you've read it,' said Chris, not very hopefully. Maitland smiled at him.

'Come now, there's no need to slander me. I gave it my most conscientious attention. But it's the first time, you know, that I've been called upon to defend a client whose name I didn't even know.'

'Tommy Smith,' said Chris, shrugging.

'You didn't tell me that.'

'No, because I didn't know it myself at first. But that's what he told the grocer he worked for as an errand boy.'

'But he refused to tell the police, or you. Which gives rise to the assumption that it may not be true.'

'I don't think for a moment it's true,' Conway told him. 'It doesn't seem very important, after all.'

'Don't you think so? I should have said it was the most important thing in the whole case.'

'Why?' asked Conway baldly.

'Because there must be some reason behind it.'

'Sheer bloody-mindedness,' Bushey suggested.

'It's a thought. Is he bloody-minded, Chris?'

Conway pondered. 'Why do you always have to ask such awkward questions?' he complained.

'It's quite simple ... yes, or no. On the evidence before us,' he added encouragingly, 'his failure to co-operate by giving his name, I should say the answer must be yes.'

'It's not quite so simple. He's a good-looking boy, well-spoken ... though you'll find his accent a bit broad, I expect. And unfailingly polite. Just—just quietly stubborn, I suppose you'd say.'

'I shouldn't say anything, not having seen the boy, but I'm willing to take your word for it. The old man he was living with—'

'Alfred Neale. He's occupied a disused nissen hut on the edge of the Town Allotments for years now; seven years, as far as we can gather. And we only assume the boy was living with him because his fingerprints were all over the place and there were schoolbooks on the table. There's also, of course, what the neighbours say.'

'That sounds conclusive enough.'

'I only meant that Tommy's never actually admitted he was living there.'

'I see. He wasn't attending school?'

'Nobody lays claim to him.'

'Wouldn't somebody have noticed, if he was about the place while the rest of his contemporaries were in class?'

'They would, I suppose. But Wilfred Curzon—he's the grocer, and don't tell me he's "hell instructed" because he's a kindly, rather dull man—Curzon says he only turned up for work out of school hours, and none of the neighbours can be found who ever saw him at the wrong sort of time.'

'How long had he been working for this kindly grocer of yours?'

'Since the middle of June.'

'What about the boys of his own age? Wasn't he any more open with them?'

'The police have talked to a few. When they spoke to him, Tommy always said he had an errand to do, or was expected home, or something like that.'

'But didn't any of them wonder—?'

'Why should they? I suppose the Grammar School boys thought he was going to St Blaise's, and the St Blaise boys thought he was going to the Modern School. Or vice versa, you know.'

13

'Doesn't it strike you that he was unnaturally careful for a boy of his age?'

'I suppose so, but—'

'A runaway ... don't you think?'

Chris sounded startled. 'He may have been related to old Neale, as far as anyone knows.'

'Yes, what is known about Neale?'

'He was seventy when he died. Lived in Arkenshaw all his schooldays, then left ... to earn his living elsewhere, I imagine. He came back seven years ago.'

'Means of support?'

'He drew his old age pension regularly, ever since he became eligible. But he had a cache of money too, tucked away in the pocket of an old suit. A matter of nearly £400.'

'No bank account?'

'None has been traced.'

'How did he come to be living in the nissen hut?'

'He just took it over, and as nobody wanted it nobody bothered to eject him. Over the years he seems to have made himself quite comfortable in a makeshift sort of way. You'll see for yourself, at least I suppose you'll want to see it.'

'Certainly I shall. The scene of the crime, isn't it?'

'That's right. I thought tomorrow—'

'After we've seen Tommy. To get back to the old man, you said they might be related.'

'Well, Alfred Neale had a sister, a couple of years older than himself. She married and left Arkenshaw. Now that Neale's dead, nobody knows what happened to her. The boy might be her grandson, I suppose.'

'In that case, why the secrecy? Enrol him in school, draw some sort of national assistance for him most likely. What could be simpler?'

'*I* don't know,' said Chris. He sounded very faintly

exasperated, as though annoyed with himself for not having foreseen the line Maitland's questions would take. 'I'm afraid I was taking it for granted; so are the police, for that matter.'

'Well, I don't think it follows. In that case, as I said before, why the secrecy?'

'Neale had become almost a recluse.'

'Had he so much influence over the boy. A boy, remember, who has withstood all the police attempts to get him to talk, not to mention your own.'

'I suppose it is queer,' said Chris thoughtfully. 'But the other thing about Neale is that he was a member—a fanatical member, so far as we can judge—of the Levellers.'

'I didn't know there were any of them left.'

'A few, here in the north at any rate. They call themselves that, but they may not be descended from the original movement, you know.'

'I see.'

'What I was going to say ... Tommy might be able to withstand mental pressure—well, we know he can—but not be ready to stand up to physical violence.'

'Was Neale violent? It doesn't follow, you know, that just because he had a reputation as a religious fanatic—'

'No, of course not. I'm only telling you what the police assume, what they're going to cite as the motive.'

'Ah, yes. The alleged burglary.'

'Speaking between ourselves,' said Chris frankly, 'you'll not have a leg to stand on if you take that line in court. Tommy left fingerprints all over the place.'

'Careless of him. Tell me about the burglary.'

'It's all in the brief.'

'In a case like this I prefer the spoken to the written word.' Bushey took his pipe out of his mouth, and Maitland turned to grin at him. 'As you are about to remark, it gives me an opportunity to heckle,' he said.

'Exactly,' said Bushey, still solemn, and resumed his puffing.

'It was one of the big houses on Brinkley Drive,' said Conway, sticking to his point. 'Robert Clayton, the house-holder, reported a breaking and entering, and the theft of three miniatures ... Holbeins.'

'Good lord! I didn't think anybody but a museum could afford things like that.'

'I suppose they would be valuable,' said Chris vaguely. 'Anyway, they—the police—found Tommy's fingerprints on the french window where entry had been effected, and other places as well, and the miniatures were hidden under his mattress in the nissen hut.'

'What does Tommy say about that?'

'Nothing at all. Well, no, to be exact he says, "I never took them". But what's the use of denying it in the face of the evidence?'

'You don't believe him then?'

'Do you?'

'I haven't seen the boy. But there must be some doubt in your mind—mustn't there?—about the murder at least, or why did you send for me? Bushey could have pulled out the pathetic stop at the trial just as effectively as I can. And the answer to that question, let me remind you,' he added, as Chris hesitated over his reply, 'is *not* in the brief.'

'It's not an easy one to answer,' said Chris, and glanced at Bushey as if for inspiration, but Bushey remained with-drawn. (Imperturbable, thought Chris, and that's why I wanted him so why should it annoy me now?) 'I don't like going into court without knowing what Tommy is hiding, because, as you say, it's obvious there's something. I suppose that's the sum of it really.'

'I see.' It was impossible to tell how he took that state-ment, but then there came a gleam of amusement into his eye. 'I'm quite looking forward to meeting our client,' he said. 'Where is he? Not in Wentworth Gaol?'

'No, they've fixed up a room for him at the Remand Home. An attic, really, but I must say they've made it quite comfortable.'

'You've had him medically examined?'

'Yes, of course, but he wouldn't talk to the psychiatrist either. Not at all. You'll get no joy out of the report.'

'What does it say?'

'There were signs of disturbance, but in the absence of any co-operation from the patient he couldn't form an opinion as to his sanity.'

'According to the doctors there always are signs of disturbance.'

'Well, in this case I think he was right. That was the one thing that really seemed to upset Tommy—both our doctor and theirs.'

'What did theirs say?'

'Much the same as our man. Anderson isn't calling him.'

'And you only recommend calling ours as a last resort?'

'That's right.'

There didn't seem to be much to say to that. 'You were saying that the police cite the burglary as the motive,' Maitland said.

'Not exactly. You see, the sequence of events was this. First the burglary on the 24th September ... well, I daresay it took place on the 23rd actually, but it was reported on the Wednesday morning. They thought it must be a boy who had broken in, or a very small man, or perhaps even a woman, but they hadn't the prints on file so they weren't much use at that stage. Then on the Friday morning, the 26th, they received an anonymous letter at police head-quarters. "If you want to know who robbed the Claytons' house on Brinkley Drive, ask the old man who lives in the nissen hut by the Town Allotments." They didn't reckon much to that, not having a signature, but of course they had to make enquiries and the matter was important, so Superintendent Morrison went round there himself and found Neale dead. While their enquiries were still going on Tommy came in, wouldn't say who he was or where he'd been, and while they were still wondering what to do with him the evidence of the fingerprints came out with the result that he was charged.'

'That's all very clear, but you still haven't got to the motive,' Maitland complained.

'Patience.' Chris was too absorbed in his narrative by now to be put off by interruptions. 'The police allege—and I must say it sounds reasonable—that Tommy did the burglary at Brinkley Drive. I don't think there can be much argument about that. Then Neale found the miniatures where he'd hidden them, and being the kind of man he was was shocked to the core—'

'He didn't even need to be a religious fanatic for that,' Bushey remarked, not apparently addressing either of his companions, but some point in the air between the two.

'—and picked up his stick to give the boy a thrashing. That'll be borne out by the medical evidence. There are weals on Tommy's back that couldn't have been made any other way.'

'Made on the day of the murder?' Maitland asked, suddenly alert.

Conway shook his head apologetically. 'Did I give you that impression? I'm sorry. At least a week, and probably two weeks before, the doctor thinks.'

'I see.'

'You will in a minute,' Chris prophesied without enthusiasm. 'The stick is a heavy one, a blackthorn, and Neale was never seen without it. The contention is that he raised it to strike the boy, but this time Tommy wasn't having any so he grabbed it with both hands as it descended, wrenched it out of the old man's grip, and proceeded to batter him to death.'

'Could he have done that?'

'Oh, yes. Neale wasn't a big man. And there are fingerprints to bear it out, two very clear sets where Tommy took hold of the stick, and then some blurs where he slid his hands further up to get a better grip.'

'And the medical evidence, I suppose, bears out that the stick was used in the murder.'

'I don't think there can be any doubt about that.'

'What does Tommy have to say?'

'Just, I didn't do it. Not very helpful.'

'I'm not so sure about that. With his capacity for silence, why should he say anything at all?'

Chris thought about that. 'Because he's frightened,' he suggested.

'I'm afraid that may be true. He denies killing Neale ... why do you always have such messy murders in Arkenshaw, Chris? And he denies stealing the miniatures. Was it just that, or did he also deny doing the break in?'

'Now you come to mention it, it was just the theft he denied.' Conway paused again, and then went on more urgently, 'You're getting ideas into your head already, Antony. That wasn't what I wanted at all.'

'Didn't you?' Antony sounded amused. 'As to Tommy's guilt or innocence my mind, I assure you, is completely open. If you really want to find out more about him though, I have a couple of suggestions to make.'

'Of course I want to know more about him!' Conway's voice rose a little, protestingly.

'All right then. First set your local bloodhounds—I don't remember their names if ever I knew them—on to finding out where Neale's sister went, and whether she's alive or dead, and what offspring ... you know the kind of thing as well as I do.'

'Will that help?'

'If the answers are constructive, it might help to force Tommy's confidence.'

'But you don't think they will be.'

'Somehow I don't. I think—' He hesitated, and then went on more positively, 'I think Tommy must have some serious reason for remaining silent, something he's afraid that we—or the police—will find out. For that reason I think you might suggest, as tactfully as possible, to who-ever's in charge of the investigation that his fingerprints should be circulated. Being a juvenile, I doubt if that's been done.'

'But—' said Chris.

Bushey removed his pipe and said thoughtfully, 'If there's anything to know, aren't you rather making a present of it to the prosecution?'

'That seems to be the price of knowledge. I think it may be more important for us to know than for them not to, if you see what I mean.'

'I don't quite like it,' said Chris, 'but I suppose, if you really think it's necessary—'

'I'm in two minds, like you. But on the whole ... yes, I think we should go ahead on those lines. Who's in charge? It will have to be someone in the detective branch, not your revered father-in-law.'

'No, of course not. Superintendent Morrison, I should think, or Inspector Thorpe if he isn't available. I'll see one of them tomorrow morning, before I call for you.'

'What time did you say we'd be at the Remand Home?'

'About ten-thirty. That gives me plenty of time.'

'Are you coming with us, Bushey?'

'Sorry, I've got to be in court. In any case,' said Bushey, unusually loquacious, 'I've a feeling I shall see as much as

I can stomach of our client during the course of the trial. I can't stand these sullen youngsters.'

'But he isn't,' said Chris quickly. Then he caught Antony's eye and smiled. 'Oh, well, you'll see for yourself,' he concluded weakly.

Star rejoined them after that, with another pot of coffee, and it was late when Antony, accepting Bushey's offer of a lift, in view of the fact that he still had his suitcase with him, arrived at the Midland Hotel and went across to the desk to register. The lobby was almost as cavern-like as the railway station, a place of Victorian solidity, with too much mahogany and brass about it, redeemed only by a number of ugly, but very comfortable, chairs. Maitland had just finished signing his name when the door of the dining-room usually dedicated to the use of the members of his profession during the assize swung open, and a group of men, some of whom he recognised, came out. Greetings were exchanged, and he found himself mounting the stairs at the rear of a small procession, in company with a large, grizzled man of perhaps sixty-five, impeccably tailored and with every hair in place ... William Anderson, with whom he would be crossing swords in court as soon as the case of Tommy 'Smith' was reached.

They went up in silence, and it was only when the rest of the party had dispersed and they were standing on the first floor landing that Anderson spoke with what his companion immediately felt was a spurious geniality. 'Well, Maitland, so we meet again.'

There wasn't much to be said to that. 'We do, indeed,' said Maitland, and waited, a little puzzled but not exactly disturbed by the other man's tone.

'I suppose,' said Anderson, 'you're expecting another easy victory.'

'Easy?' said Antony. His first emotion was surprise, but then he couldn't help feeling a certain wry amusement. 'I

21

wouldn't have called it easy, and I wouldn't have called it a victory exactly. If you're talking about what happened when Joe Hartley was tried, that is.'

'What else?' There was no doubt about it now, some animosity lay behind the casually spoken words. 'Are you going to try for a verdict of manslaughter again?'

'If the facts seem to justify it, yes.' The justice of what had happened in that former case had seemed so self-evident to him that it had never occurred to him that his opponent might have taken a different view. 'I only arrived this evening,' he added, 'and I haven't even seen my client yet.'

'Much good may it do you!'

'Precisely.' Maitland, with intent to annoy, beamed at him. 'A chap after my own heart,' he said enthusiastically. 'I've always wanted to defend someone who knew when to keep his mouth shut.'

'I hope you'll continue to feel so pleased about it,' said Anderson, which was manifestly a lie. He hesitated a moment, then said, 'Good night,' rather curtly and turned away down the corridor. Antony found the night porter waiting with his suitcase, and followed him in the opposite direction to his own room.

Here, even his surroundings were evocative ... the dark paint, the heavy mahogany furniture, the bed whose springs creaked protestingly as he sat down on it; the room a little too cold for comfort, just as the bathroom, he knew from experience, would be too warm. He never came to Arkenshaw, it seemed, but his mind was in a turmoil, and now there was the added discomfort of Anderson's attitude. As Counsel for the Prosecution he would, of course, present his case with skill, but if there was added to that some genuine animosity towards the Defence ...

'It isn't worth thinking about,' said Antony aloud to himself. But the shadow was there, and it wasn't going to

22

be dispelled as easily as all that. Even after he had talked to Jenny he was still feeling ruffled, and it was a long time before he slept.

I

It wasn't as bad as prison visiting, but the Remand Home was a dour looking building, and even the pleasantly furnished attic room that had been allotted to the prisoner couldn't make Maitland forget altogether that the door was locked. But it was no time, he told himself rather impatiently, to be considering his own feelings. There must be some way of making the boy talk.

To his eye, Chris was palpably nervous, but nobody else would have noticed it, certainly not Tommy. Or would he? As Conway meandered on, more discursive than usual ('This is Mr Maitland, your counsel, I explained to you last time I saw you what that meant'), Antony was taking stock of his client. Tommy was outwardly self-possessed; tall for his age, and reed thin, with wrists and ankles protruding bonily from a neat, rather dreadful, blue serge suit. He was brown eyed and oval faced, and had dark hair, rather unruly, that looked as if it had been given, at no very distant date, a pudding-basin, do-it-yourself cut. He didn't seem to be giving more attention to Chris than politeness demanded, but was weighing up the stranger with unashamed curiosity.

Tommy saw a tall man, with dark hair and grey eyes, who was serious enough at the moment but who looked as if most things would amuse him, given half a chance. He had a casual, friendly air which the boy distrusted instinctively; he wasn't inclined, just then, to take anyone at their face value.

Perhaps this scrutiny was no more than could be expected. What was less expected was that Tommy should say, as soon as Chris had finished speaking, 'I suppose you want to ask me some more questions. Hasn't Mr Conway explained to you that I've nowt to say?' His accent was broad, as Chris had warned, but Antony, who had a good ear which had already become to some degree adjusted to the local accent, found no difficulty in following him.

He said now, lightly, 'I'm sure we can find something to talk about.' And then, glancing at Chris, 'I daresay we'd better all sit down.' For himself he would have preferred to remain standing, to be free to roam about the room at will, but he didn't want to do anything to distract Tommy's attention from their conversation. So he took a straight-backed, tweed-upholstered chair and watched the others emulate him, and then went on, still as casually as he could, 'How long had you been living with Mr Neale in the nissen hut?'

There was some hesitation about that. 'I never said I'd ever lived there.'

'Come now, that's one of the few things we do know about you. It isn't exactly incriminating,' said Antony, and then wondered whether he should have chosen a shorter word. But Tommy took it in his stride, and perhaps even may have found it reassuring, for he said quite readily, though after a doubtful glance at Chris Conway,

'All right then. I was staying with him.'

'For how long?'

'Quite a long time.'

'Couldn't you be a little more exact about it?' That earned a shake of the head, but no reply. 'Weeks, months, years? There surely can't be any harm in telling us that.'

'No good either.' There was nothing rude about his tone, but he seemed to feel some apology was called for. 'I'm sorry, when you've come all the way from London. Mr Conway should have explained to you—'

'Oh, he did. But I hoped, you see, that now you'd had time to think things over ... it's very hard to help you, you know, when we've nothing to base our defence on.'

'It wouldn't help,' said Tommy positively.

'Won't you let me be the judge of that?'

'I'm sorry, it wouldn't help, I know it wouldn't.'

'You had been working for Mr Curzon, the grocer, since the middle of June.'

'Yes.' He sounded cautious, as if even this grudging admission might somehow entrap him.

'What did you do before that? Did you work for anybody else?' That didn't get a reply at all, unless a very slight shake of the head could be taken as implying a negative. 'Well then, tell me about Mr Neale. How did you get on with him?'

'We got on all right.'

'What sort of man was he?'

'Just an ordinary sort of chap.'

'There were schoolbooks in the hut. Who bought those?'

'He did.' He smiled suddenly, and oddly enough it was at this moment that Maitland realised fully for the first time that the apparent self-possession was only a very thin veneer, covering what might easily become panic fear. 'Put me through a proper sort of exam before he bought them, too.'

'To see how far you had reached in your studies?'

'That's right.'

'Was he able to help you?'

'With English, and History, and Geography ... things like that. Not with Maths, not really, though he sometimes studied the problems along with me and helped me that way.'

'Not a completely uneducated man, then?'

'Oh, no. He was getting books all the time from the library and reading them.'

'What sort of books?'

'Philosophy, he said. I didn't understand them much. And biography sometimes, which was rather a bore because he used to get worked up about other people's sins.'

'He was a religious man, wasn't he? Or so I've been told.'

'Yes, frightfully. We used to go to chapel twice on Sundays. That's why he bought me this suit, for best. I had shorts and a sweater to wear during the week.'

'Shorts and a sweater of your own.' His tone was still casual, but the question brought Tommy up short.

'I—I didn't say that.'

'That's why I asked you, to get matters clear between us.'

'Well, he bought them at the same time,' said Tommy, in such a rush that the words were slurred together.

'Can you show them to me?'

'No.'

'Why not? Didn't they bring all your clothes when you came here?'

'Yes, but she took them away. Matron did.'

'Then, if I ask her—'

'I think she burned them. She said they weren't fit to wear.'

'I see. How long had you been going to chapel with Mr Neale?'

'For ages.'

'That's something I can find out for myself, you know. I shall be talking to the minister.'

Tommy took no notice of this, but changed the subject. It might have been a deliberate action on his part, or it might not. 'When will I have to go to court?' he asked. He was still trying, without and very great success, to hide his anxiety.

'Perhaps Mr Conway can tell us that.'

'I think perhaps it may be tomorrow, Tommy. There's

27

nothing to be afraid of, you know,' said Chris gently.

'They won't lock me up again when it's over. Of course they will!' His tone was desperate, and Antony had deliberately to harden his heart. It wasn't pleasant, taking advantage of a boy's fear, and one besides that was so well founded.

'If you'd answer my questions frankly we might be able to help you, Mr Conway and I.'

'It wouldn't help. You don't understand. It wouldn't help.'

'I can't understand, can I, unless you tell me—?'

'It wouldn't help,' said Tommy again, despairingly.

'Well, you may as well tell me how long you've been going to chapel with Mr Neale, because I can find out quite easily,' Maitland pointed out.

'All right then.' Tommy sounded sulky now. 'Ever since June.'

'Was that when you first went to live with him?' As there was no reply to that he went on thoughtfully, 'I think it must have been. He made you keep up with your studies. He'd never have let you off chapel attendance, would he?'

'Think what you like,' He had got command of himself again now; there was resignation in his tone, rather than rudeness.

'Thank you. I will. At least there can be no harm in telling me about your life with him. Or can there?'

'It was nothing out of the way.'

'Tell me.' Maitland's tone was quietly insistent.

'There's nowt to tell.'

'During the school holidays you went out as you liked, I suppose.'

'More or less. I had errands to do for Mr Curzon, but *he* liked me to be in at night.'

'Who? Mr Neale?'

'Yes, of course. When school started again I had to

28

study, and I did the errands around tea time. When I got paid I used to get the groceries ... bread, and milk, and marge, and things in tins mostly. He wasn't much of a cook, except to warm a tin of soup or something like that, and he wouldn't let me try. He said it was "all vanity", but I don't know what he meant.'

That was the longest speech so far, but Maitland wasn't optimistic enough to see it as a sign that the boy was relaxing his guard. 'Why didn't you go to school with the other boys?' he asked.

It nearly worked. 'Because—' said Tommy, and clamped his lips together and gave him a wary look.

'Because Tommy Smith was a good enough name to give to a casual employer, but a school would have wanted to know something about your background, wouldn't they?'

'I just don't like going to school,' said Tommy defiantly.

'Just a whim of yours, in fact?'

'That's right.'

'And Mr Neale went along with it. He took you in and looked after you, but he demanded obedience, didn't he? Yet for some reason he never insisted on your going to school.'

'He made me work at home.'

'That's not quite the same thing. As a disciplinary measure ... did he often beat you?'

'No.'

'He did once though, didn't he?'

'Yes, he did.'

'Why.'

'Because I went for a walk one Sunday evening, and he couldn't find me when it was time to go to chapel.'

'Why did you stay with him? You'd run away once, hadn't you?'

Tommy made no attempt to answer the second part of that question, but it soon became obvious that he was giving the first part careful consideration. 'I don't know,' he said at last, slowly. 'I suppose it was just because I needed somebody who cared what happened to me.'

There was a plea for understanding there and Antony was again aware of that unmilling stab of sympathy. 'If it makes any difference, there's Mr Conway here who cares quite a lot what happens to you,' he said. 'And so do I, for that matter.'

'Yes ... well ... I can't very well run away this time, can I?' Afterwards Antony was to think that this had probably been intended as an essay in humour, but Tommy shivered involuntarily as he spoke, so that his counsel was again overcome by distaste for the job he had undertaken. It would have been so much easier to tackle if his sympathies hadn't been aroused.

'They're being kind to you, aren't they?' he asked. 'The warders who stay with you, I mean.'

'Oh, yes.' As if he felt he had in some way betrayed himself, Tommy was nonchalant again. 'But I sometimes feel they don't think of me as a person at all, just a job of work.'

'I wouldn't mind betting you're wrong about that,' said Antony seriously. For some reason it seemed important to convince the boy of the truth of what he said. Because there wasn't just the watching, the lack of privacy, but the turn of the key in the lock ... with its reminder of, perhaps, a multitude of such days ahead. If the boy had indeed been a lay figure, how easy it would have been! But he was living, breathing, feeling with all the passion of which he was capable, that was painfully obvious. And he was frightened by the prospect of what lay ahead of him, that was obvious too. Maitland got up, no longer thinking what he was doing, and began to walk up and down the room behind the circle of chairs that surrounded the gas fire. For the first time he was really facing up to the question of his client's guilt or innocence, because if he was innocent ...

'Did you kill Alfred Neale?' he shot at him abruptly.

'I didn't!' Tommy sounded more indignant than anything else. 'I thought you and Mr Conway were supposed to believe me about that, whatever anybody else did.' It wasn't until later that it occurred to Antony that this was rather an odd reaction.

Now he said, half humorously, 'You're not giving us very much encouragement, are you? All this secrecy.'

'But it wouldn't help, it really wouldn't.'

'Don't you think we should be the best judges of that.'

Tommy didn't attempt to reply to that, only shook his head dejectedly. 'Oh, very well!' said Maitland impatiently after a moment. 'Tell us instead where you were when the police discovered Neale's body.'

'I was out.'

'Where?'

'Just ... out.'

'You went out for a walk rather than stay in the hut with his body?'

'It wasn't like that. I didn't know—'

That was only too obviously an unfinished sentence. As abruptly as he had started, Maitland stopped his pacing again. 'What didn't you know?' he asked, very softly.

Tommy kept his head turned away, and would not meet his counsel's eye. 'I didn't know he was dead,' he said, and sounded, oddly, ashamed of what he was saying.

'I see. You'd been out all night then?'

'I—' The boy looked up then, and for the first time there was some colour in his cheeks. 'I think you're trying to be kind to me, Mr Maitland. I don't want to tell you lies.'

'So you'd rather stay mute. There's a phrase in law, Tommy, which you won't have heard, "mute of malice". I used to think it was rather an unfair description of someone who didn't want to plead, but now I'm beginning to wonder.'

'I'm not ... I can't ... anyway, you wouldn't believe me.' Tommy was desperate again.

'Try me.'

'No.' But he lowered his eyes again, and seemed to become conscious for the first time that his fists were clenched tightly. He unclenched them, and leaned back in his chair, relaxing deliberately.

Antony took a turn about the room and came back to stand behind the chair he had originally occupied and say, casual again, 'Mr Conway tells me you didn't deny breaking into the house on Brinkley Crescent.'

'He told me it was no use denying it, because there were fingerprints.'

'So you made a virtue of necessity.' Tommy looked up and smiled rather shyly, responding to the tone, probably, rather than to the words. 'Why did you go there?'

'Not to steal! They didn't find my fingerprints on those —those little pictures, because I never touched them.'

'They had been wiped clean,' said Chris, setting the record straight.

'But not by me. I never stole anything. I wouldn't! It's a mean thing to do.'

'Why then did you go to Brinkley Crescent?'

'I ... had a reason.'

'So I suppose.' He heard an echo of Sir Nicholas in his tone, and pulled himself up on the instant. (But Uncle Nick had been gentleness itself, the only time he had heard him examining a child.) 'What I want you to tell me, Tommy, is what that reason was.'

'I'm not telling you. That's another thing you wouldn't believe, and anyway—'

'What?' said Maitland as he paused.

'—it'd be like telling tales.'

There ought to be some clue in that statement. 'Did you know any of the boys round about?'.

'Not to say know. I talked to them sometimes.'

'Do you know who they were?'

'Only first names. John, and Mark, and Simon.'

'It doesn't matter,' said Chris, breaking in again. 'I know them.'

But Antony wasn't listening. 'Did somebody *dare* you to break into the Clayton's house?' he asked.

'I—' Tommy hesitated. 'Yes, that was it, it was a dare.'

'How would your friends know you'd been there? Didn't you have to take something to show them?'

'They'd take my word.'

'Tommy, you said you wouldn't lie to me.'

'I didn't say that! Did I, Mr Conway? I said I didn't *want* to lie to you.'

'Yes, there's a difference, isn't there? I wonder if you understand, Tommy, what will happen at your trial.'

'Mr Conway told me something about it ... about the judge, and that.'

'Did he explain to you that there would be counsel appointed—men in the same line of business as I am—to put the case against you to the court?'

'He told me that too.'

'But do you understand, I wonder, the strength of the case against you.'

'I ... yes, I understand that all right.' There was the faintest tremor in his voice now.

'So what do you think we're going to be doing while that is going on?'

'I thought you sort of took it in turns.'

'Not altogether. I have the opportunity of questioning the prosecution witnesses ... that's called cross-examination. But don't you see, Tommy, when it comes to my turn you're leaving me without anything to say on your behalf?'

'I didn't kill him.'

'That statement will be covered by your plea of Not Guilty. It doesn't go very far, does it?'

'No,' said Tommy, unwillingly, 'I suppose it doesn't.'

'It's even a hindrance, in a way. If you admitted to striking him we might make something of a plea of self defence.'

'I don't ... I'm sorry, Mr Maitland, I don't quite understand that.'

'No, I suppose you don't.' He exchanged a glance with Conway, and Chris shook his head slightly. 'The prosecution will say, you see, that Neale was angry when he saw you had stolen the miniatures and came towards you with his stick raised to give you another beating. But you grabbed at the stick and got it away from him—'

He broke off there. Every vestige of colour had drained from Tommy's cheeks. He said—it was no more than a whisper, not meant to be overheard—'So that's how—' and stopped in his turn and looked from his counsel to his solicitor, wide-eyed. 'None of that happened,' he protested. 'But if it had, it wouldn't make any difference to grown-up people. They'd think I deserved all I got and should have let him beat me if he wanted to.'

'We could at least try to enlighten them,' said Maitland soberly.

'It wouldn't do any good. Anyway, I didn't—'

'There are your fingerprints on the stick,' said Conway, in his quiet way. He always had a fondness for facts; which came in useful, Maitland knew, when he himself was indulging in one of his flights of fancy.

'I've been living with him. I must have touched it a hundred times.'

'Why?'

'To hand it to him, I suppose. Or if it was in the way when I was sweeping the floor.'

34

'Neale was never seen without his stick. Didn't he keep it equally close at hand when he was in the hut?'

'Yes, but ... not always. I don't remember exactly, but there must have been times—'

'That will be pointed out to the court, of course,' Maitland told him. 'But it's surmise, not evidence.'

'If I'd done it, why should I have gone back to the hut again?'

'I don't know, but I can guess what the prosecution's answer to that will be. You were going to run away again, but you needed money. Did you know there was nearly £400 hidden in the pocket of an old suit?'

'I knew he had something put away, but not that it was as much as that.' He looked again from one of them to the other, and then tugged a handkerchief from his pocket and dabbed angrily at his eyes. 'I thought you were on my side. I thought you *had* to believe me, whatever I told you,' he said.

'It isn't quite so simple. We're on your side, certainly, but believing you is another matter. You're not giving us very much to go on, are you?'

'If I answered every question you've asked me, it wouldn't do any good,' said Tommy gloomily.

'There are four main points,' said Antony, ignoring this. 'What is your name? Why were you hiding out here, in effect, not attending school, refusing to talk about your former life? Why did you break into the house in Brinkley Crescent? And where the devil were you when the murder was committed and for the rest of the night? If you'd tell me the answer to those, Tommy lad, I'd be a happier man.'

'Well, I'm sorry.' Tommy paused to blow his nose and stuff the handkerchief back in his pocket again. 'I don't want to seem ungrateful to—to either of you, but I—I can't tell you those things.'

And though they went backwards and forwards over the

same ground for more than an hour after that, they were still no further forward when they rapped on the door for the warder to let them out of the room.

II

They had lunch at a nearby pub; there is always a nearby pub in Arkenshaw, and usually its interior is polished and sparkling to a degree that rebukes its dour surroundings. Over a ploughman's lunch they concocted a plan of campaign. 'We'll take a view of the old boy's hut first,' said Chris. 'Then I can go back to the office and take care of a few odds and ends there while you go and see Grandma, if that's really the next item on your agenda.'

'It is.'

'We're going there for supper tomorrow night, I told you that.'

'So you did. I shall be delighted to see Inspector Duckett again, but just now it's the old lady I want to talk to.'

'I believe you look on her as a—as a sort of mascot,' said Chris in a grumbling tone.

Antony laughed, but he seemed to be giving the remark his serious consideration. 'She's always been of the greatest help to me,' he said. 'I suppose I've got a superstitious feeling—'

'Better not let her hear you say that,' Chris advised. 'She'd be down on you like a ton of bricks.'

'So she would. However, I've an excellent sense of self-preservation, you really needn't worry about me at all.'

'I won't! Then if you want to talk to the three boys Tommy mentioned, by the time you've had tea with Grandma they'll be out of school.'

'Yes, I suppose that is the obvious thing. There's this minister chap though.'

'Mr Harte. Later this evening. Are you thinking of calling him? There are dangers about that, I should have thought.'

'If he gets up in the witness box and says Neale was a religious maniac—'

'He's not likely to do that, the old boy was a pillar of his chapel. That doesn't sound right, exactly, but you know what I mean.'

'All the same, if Anderson asks him what Neale would have done if he found the boy he was sheltering was a thief, his answer's likely to bolster the prosecution's case, don't you think?'

'So long as we proceed with the Not Guilty plea, that's what I'm afraid of. Of course, he might be willing to put in a good word for Tommy.'

'Well, damn it all, Chris, what *are* we going to do? We haven't even the beginnings of a case, I've never felt so completely at a loss.'

'What do you think, now that you've seen our client?'

'He's an interesting boy, lots of strength of character. I didn't enjoy hounding him.'

'That wasn't what I meant.'

'No, you meant did he kill Neale or didn't he? I haven't the faintest idea. He says he didn't.'

'Yes, but he denies stealing the miniatures too. And that quite obviously is a lie.'

'I wonder.'

'Now, Antony—'

'They'll be calling the owner—what's his name?—to give evidence, won't they?'

'Robert Clayton. Yes, he's being called by the prosecution.'

'Now, there's a chap I'd like a chance to talk to, without having Anderson interrupting every second word, and ... who's the judge?'

'Gilmour.'

'No!' Mr Justice Gilmour could be awkward when he liked, as he generally did. 'Well, it'll be no use his asking questions about this business, will it? Because I don't know the answers myself.'

'Why are you so interested in Clayton?'

'Because if Tommy does happen to be telling the truth—'

'What then?'

'I don't know. I wish I did.' He drank the last of his beer and put down the tankard regretfully. 'Time to be off, Chris. We've got a full day ahead of us.'

III

The Town Allotments covered an area of about two acres and were, almost without exception, carefully tended. This was the north-west side of the city, a district of grey terrace houses, some of them with gaily painted front doors, and most of them with thresholds carefully whitened and the curtains at the parlour window starched and clean. It was difficult to see what purpose the nissen hut had originally served, but it had been there so long that it seemed to blend into the landscape. The door had a new looking padlock. 'The police put that there,' said Chris, producing a key. 'Neale never bothered to lock up.'

'With four hundred quid in the place, and perhaps more originally?'

'I imagine he thought his frugal way of life was sufficient protection. Nobody would guess there was anything of value here.'

'I suppose not.'

Chris had the padlock open by now, and swung the door ajar. It was dim inside the hut, though the windows were fairly clean. 'I think he had a cleanliness is next to godliness

38

thing,' said Chris, as Antony stood looking about him. 'Of course, it's been searched and fingerprinted and generally messed about, but Morrison told me it was pretty spruce originally.'

The hut was divided into two, the one they were in being the larger section, and a curtain that looked as if it had originally been a kitchen table-cloth hanging in the doorway that led to the inner room. There was a table with a scrubbed top and some books piled carelessly on it. 'Due back at the library from the looks of it,' said Antony, glancing at them. 'Does Tommy have anything to read, by the way, I forgot to ask him.'

'The police had taken him his schoolbooks, but I don't think he was in a mood for those,' said Chris, coming up beside him. 'I got him a set of Sir Walter Scott, he can't possibly have got through them all yet.'

'Is he a reader? I hope so, for his own sake.'

'He fell on them with some enthusiasm, as a matter of fact. I daresay Neale thought novels were snares of the devil, and wouldn't let him have them.'

'I can see you're going to be a corrupting influence.' Mailand's tone was absent. There was a straight chair pushed under the table, a kitchen chair lacking most of its paint; an armchair in an advanced state of decrepitude pulled close to the iron stove, on which stood a battered tin kettle, and which had a long poker and a shovel propped up against it. A cupboard in the corner—again scrubbed almost free of paint—held a saucepan, some odd items of crockery and cutlery, a mouldy loaf and some tinned goods, and a small store of candles. A curtain on a sagging wire, which hung across another corner, concealed cleaning materials; a tin trunk contained a few items of clothing, and had a chipped enamel basin on top of it which had apparently done duty both for washing and for washing up. 'He got his water from a tap outside,' said Chris, indicating a red plastic bucket, the one gaudy thing in that cheerless room. 'He kept a little coke in a lean-to outside, but that's gone by now, I bet.'

'An austere sort of existence,' Antony agreed, as he crossed the room to pull back the dividing curtain. There was a bed on each side of the inner chamber, each of them consisting of two or three old mattresses piled together. They had faded coverlets, but seemed to be neatly made. A wooden crate, upturned, served as a table, but there was nothing on it but a single candle. The two windows in here were curtained, as were the four windows in the larger room, with cheap print material, carelessly tacked together. 'Is that all the light they had?' asked Maitland. 'Surely—'

'There was an oil lamp in the other room, and a can of fuel. The Superintendent took them away ... thought if the local kids get in through the windows—and they will get in sooner or later, you can be sure of that—they might set the place on fire and not find it so easy to get out again.'

'I see. A thoughtful chap, your Superintendent Morrison. What did he say to you this morning?'

'He said he'd circulate Tommy's fingerprints, as requested; but he gave me a queerish sort of look, I can tell you.'

'I'm not altogether surprised.'

'It was your idea,' Chris pointed out, without heat.

'I hadn't forgotten. Well, thank you for bringing me here, Chris, but I don't think it has told us much, has it?'

'Not a thing.'

'Except perhaps that Tommy must have been pretty desperate for somewhere to stay.'

'I don't know so much about that. It would be no worse than camping out, and to a boy—'

'I daresay you're right.' Maitland interrupted him rather quickly. 'But there's also the fact that he was made to go to chapel twice on Sundays, which to most normal boys ...

don't tell me Neale had converted him too.'

'I should think it's unlikely.'

'He was frightened ... don't you think?'

'Does that surprise you?'

'I don't mean *now*, that's obvious. I mean he was frightened of facing the world alone, and that's why he stayed with Neale, which reinforces my idea that he was running away from something, wouldn't you say?'

'I think you're going too far, too fast,' said Conway candidly.

'Ah, well, who lives may learn.' Antony sounded resigned. 'I've had enough of this singularly depressing place, Chris. How do I get to Old Peel Farm from here?'

'I'll take you.'

'But you want to get back to the office.'

'It would take the rest of the afternoon to get there by bus, and you won't pick up a taxi around here.'

'Thank you, then. You know, Chris,' he added, as they walked back to the car, 'when Tommy said he couldn't tell us where he was the night Neale was killed, I thought for a moment he was going to say "I daren't"?'

But when Chris tried to pursue the subject, he seemed disinclined to elaborate on the remark.

IV

Old Peel Farm, where Star Conway's father and grandmother lived, stood on high ground on the outskirts of the town, with a high wall bounding the Arkenshaw Waterworks property in front of it, and a golf course behind. That day, in the October sunshine, it looked mellow and friendly, and when Antony had watched Chris drive away he went up the flagged path to the front door without any hesitation at all, sure of his welcome.

Not that he expected there would be anything effusive in Grandma Duckett's greeting, he knew her too well for that. When, after a little delay, she opened the door to him she said only, 'So it's you,' and added, almost grudgingly, 'you'd best come in.' But when she had closed the door carefully and led the way into the kitchen, there was a small table set with tea things pulled close to her favourite Windsor chair. Two cups and saucers, Antony noted.

'You're expecting somebody,' he said. 'I'd better go.'

That brought Grandma's rather grim smile. 'I thought as how 'appen you'd be coming,' she told him.

'You couldn't have known.'

'That Chris said you'd be busy all day,' she agreed, not without some satisfaction in her tone. She was a stiff-backed, stout old lady, with creamy-white hair drawn into a tight bun, a roseleaf complexion, and blue eyes that had a very direct way of looking at you. 'If you'd read your horoscope this morning,' she said now, seating herself and waving a hand in invitation towards a chair at the other side of the hearth, 'you'd have known that it was a bad day for business, but a good day for looking up old friends.'

There was more encouragement in that than he would have dared to expect. 'I'm glad of that, anyway,' he said. 'As for "business", stars or no, you're just about right.'

Grandma gave him a keen look. 'You're worried again,' she said roughly.

'Is it so very obvious?' He sounded despondent, and she answered him in a bracing tone.

'No more than I expected. You're affected by Mercury, you know, as well as by t' moon.'

'Is that such a bad thing?' he asked warily.

'It means you've no more sense than to take other people's troubles on your shoulders, think on,' said Grandma in a scolding voice.

42

That made him smile. 'It's all very well, but that's what I'm paid for, after all,' he said.

'Stuff and nonsense!' said Grandma, energetically. 'Still, now you're here you may as well mash t' tea. It's all ready in t' pot.'

Because of the war-time injury to his shoulder, which still limited the use of his right arm, he had to take up the heavy iron kettle awkwardly, in his left hand, but at this stage in their acquaintance the old lady knew better than to make any comment on this. She looked down instead at her own hands, which were twisted with arthritis, and did not look up again until the kettle was back on the bars of the range, and the teapot safely on the warm ledge above the fire. Then she said, 'Leave it stand a minute, to draw.' This didn't surprise him. The brew would be strong enough to take the skin off the roof of your mouth, but he never yet had courage enough to refuse it.

'It isn't really nonsense,' he said, just as if their conversation hadn't been interrupted by the process of tea-making.

'You've defended murder cases before,' Grandma pointed out. It was just as well he had expected no sympathy, for there was none in her tone; but, almost insensibly, the cloud of oppression that afflicted him was lifting. 'What's so different about it this time?'

'Hasn't Chris told you?'

'If you mean it's a boy you're defending, that's nothing to get sentimental about.'

'I'm not!' said Maitland indignantly.

'Boys are tough. Most boys,' she amended after a moment's reflection, and gave him a baleful look.

'Well this one ... I don't know. He said, "I think you're trying to be kind to me." Heaven and earth! If I can't make a better impression than that on a boy who's frightened I ought to change my profession ... don't you

43

think? And then I reduced him to tears.'

The old lady seemed to be considering this. 'I reckon nowt to that. If he's frightened it's none of your doing,' she said at length, reasonably.

'I know that.' He watched as she struggled to her feet and began to pour the tea. 'As far as I can see everybody's falling over backwards to be kind to him, but it's so difficult for the authorities to deal with a child his age. With the best will in the world there are problems that are almost insurmountable.'

'It doesn't help, you know, worrying yourself sick.' She handed him a cup filled almost to the brim with a sinister, dark brown liquid, and he set it down on the ledge in front of the oven. When she had seated herself again she added thoughtfully, 'What's he like then, this lad of yours?'

'A nice looking boy, well spoken, polite ... damnably stubborn.'

'Even if he is, there's no call for you to be swearing about it, Mr Maitland,' said Grandma severely. But after a moment, seeing no lightening of his downcast look, she relented a little. 'Come now, it's not like you to sit there without a word to say for yourself, choose 'ow.'

'We've no case, Grandma, no case at all. Unless we could try to get the plea reduced to one of manslaughter.'

'Like you did with Joe Hartley.'

'That's right. (But there wasn't really much comparison, was there? Joe Hartley had been older, and in any case had never denied that he had killed his foster father; the only trouble had been that he wouldn't say why.) And there's another thing, when we get into court I'm afraid Tommy may be going to suffer for my sins.'

'What's that supposed to mean?'

'Anderson—he's prosecuting—is hostile.'

'Isn't that his job?'

44

'Not to press his case more than is reasonable. But he seems to think I put one over on him somehow over the Hartley affair, and one way and another he's not loving me very much at the moment. If I had a case to offer the court I could cope with that, but as things are he's going to have everything his own way.'

'The judge wouldn't let him bully t' lad, would he?'

'There's no question of that. With Tommy not answering questions there's nothing to be gained by calling him as a witness.'

'Chris was hoping he'd talk to you.'

'Well, he didn't, not about anything that matters. You have to admire him really. He knows exactly how far he wants to go, and he won't go one step farther.'

'That sounds like wicked obstinacy to me.'

'I don't know. I don't know why, you see. Who's to know what goes on in the head of a thirteen-year-old?'

'You said you might try to get t' plea reduced.' Grandma produced the phrase doubtfully, as if she wasn't sure she was remembering it correctly.

'Yes, that would arise naturally out of the prosecution's own case. But the trouble is, you see, we'd have to put Tommy into the witness box to tell his own story, and I can't even get him to admit he killed the old man.'

'Perhaps he didn't.' The old lady was sipping her tea, but her eyes were on Maitland's face, and she wasn't surprised when he threw out his hand in a vague, dissatisfied gesture and said gloomily,

'That's half the trouble, Grandma. I'm not a bit sure, either way.'

'From what Fred tells me, t' evidence is very clear.'

'Yes, but there's the boy himself. You've heard about the burglary?'

'I have.'

'Well, he admits breaking into the Claytons' house, but he absolutely denies taking the miniatures. And he says he didn't kill Neale, either.'

Old Mrs Duckett didn't answer this directly. After a pause she said instead, reminiscently, 'I remember when you were fair mockraffled as to what our Fred had been up to.'

At any other time the unfamiliar word might have provided a change of subject. Now he was as intent upon their conversation as he might have been upon a witness in court. 'Yes, but ... you put me on the right path that time,' he said. 'I remember that, too.'

'Nay, if you're worried about this Tommy you'd best carry on and see what happens.'

'I suppose that's the only thing to do. But I swear to you, Grandma, there are less leads to follow ... no, you don't like me swearing, do you? I'm sorry. What I'm trying to say is that Tommy has all the answers, and if he won't talk—'

'Something'll 'appen turn up,' said Grandma philosophically.

'Yes, well, I wondered ... had you heard of Neale before this case came up.'

'He was a character, he was. Everybody in Arkenshaw had heard of him.'

'What, for instance?'

'He was a very religious man. I wouldn't have you think I was against that myself, Mr Maitland, but those Levellers ... they aren't quite the thing.' Grandma, as he knew, combined her belief in astrology with a staunch adherence to the Methodist faith; she must feel strongly about the Levellers, because it was the nearest he had ever heard her come to criticising another person or organisation without a good deal of leverage being applied first.

'I'd got it all wrong, you know,' he said seriously. 'I

46

didn't think they were a religion, I thought they were a political party.'

'That may be how they started,' said the old lady darkly. 'They're still republicans, someone told me. Up to no good, I'll be bound.'

'Is that all you know of Neale?'

'Well ... yes,' she said, and immediately went on to contradict herself. 'People thought it was queer, him taking over that hut of his; but nobody wanted it, so no-one raised any objection. The children used to tease him, and some of the young ones reckoned to be scared of him, when he chased them waving his stick. But he never did any harm to anybody, that I heard.'

'Was that the first you heard of him, when he appropriated the hut?' She didn't answer immediately, and after a moment he went on. 'Chris said he came from Arkenshaw ... or if he didn't actually say it he implied it, I think.'

'I remember the family, 'way back,' said Grandma.

'Then tell me about them ... please!'

'What good will that do you, Mr Maitland?'

'I don't know. None probably. But if Tommy didn't kill him—'

'So you really have your doubts about that.'

'I told you—'

'So you did. Drink your tea while it's hot,' she commanded, and picked up her own cup and drank slowly, and with obvious enjoyment.

It was good advice, because somehow the hell-brew didn't taste quite so bad scalding hot as it did if you let it cool a little. So he picked up his cup and sipped delicately; Grandma would tell him in her own time, in her own way, and no use trying to hurry her, or get out of her anything which she classed under the heading of 'scurrilous talk'.

When she was satisfied that he was obeying her, she set down her cup and went on of her own accord. 'They lived

47

not too far from here, at upper end of Cargate. I went to school with his sister, Elsie, if that interests you, but there was some sort of trouble at home and she left early. Years afterwards I heard she was married, and had left town.'

'What sort of trouble?' asked Antony hopefully.

'Nothing to do with Alfred, if that's what you're thinking,' said Grandma in a dampening tone. But she added, seeing something of stubbornness in his expression, 'Their mother was proper poorly.'

'If you mean she'd taken to drink—' said Antony, guessing wildly.

'I didn't say so, Mr Maitland. Alfred would only be about eleven at the time, and all I remember about him is that he was clever with his hands. Used to do paintings of flowers and such, beautiful they were; Elsie used to bring them to show us, she was that proud of him. He went right through school, as far as I know, and then I heard he'd left town too, and never another word of him until someone told me he'd come back and was living by t' Town Allotments.'

'Didn't you wonder what he was living on?'

'It was none of my business, Mr Maitland, and anyway he'd be due for his old age pension by then. It'd be cheap living in t' hut, and no-one likely to disturb him as long as he behaved himself. And that's *all* I can tell you about him, *or* his family,' she added, in a tone that left him in no doubt at all that she meant what she said.

'What about the Claytons, then ... the people who own the miniatures Tommy is supposed to have stolen?'

'*What* about them?' said Grandma unhelpfully.

'I thought perhaps ... had you ever heard of them before you read their name in the papers over this affair?'

'Nothing to their discredit, if that's what you mean.'

'No, but ... anything, Grandma. Anything at all.'

'Robert Clayton's a well known man,' said Grandma,

relenting. 'A fine man. Chief Surgeon at St Mark's Hospital.'

'The miniatures must have been in the way of family heirlooms; something like that.'

'T' family never had any brass that I heard of.'

'Then—'

'Everybody knows Mr Clayton is a collector. House must be like a museum, from all they say. It's not what I'd like,' said Grandma, 'but no harm in it after all. There's bits in the paper every now and then, when he buys something new.'

'But surely ... even on what a *Chief* Surgeon earns—'

'He's married,' said Grandma flatly.

'Oh, I see.'

'Married a girl from Harrogate, Winnie Spencer,' said Grandma, and picked up her cup again and drank what remained of her tea. 'A fine lady,' she added then, and like her comment on the husband it was just a plain statement of fact, with no trace of envy or scorn in her voice.

'I see,' said Maitland again.

'Is that all?' she asked him. This time her tone might have been thought sarcastic. 'Always full of questions, you are,' she grumbled.

'I'm sorry.' Antony finished his tea, and put down the cup thankfully. 'If you don't mind another question, how is Inspector Duckett? I saw Star and the baby last night, you know.'

Their talk drifted comfortably to family matters, and by the time Maitland asked permission to phone for a taxi, and went through into Inspector Duckett's chilly little office to do so, it was already later than he had intended.

V

The three boys who had had, or attempted to have some communication with Tommy, all lived in the same neat terrace of houses, not far from the Town Allotments. John Thorpe was twelve, small for his age, with ginger hair and freckles, and something of the refined toughness of a youthful James Cagney. His chosen companions were both fourteen years old; Mark Dickinson was tallish and slim, and Simon Fell was tallish and fat, but even with these differences between them Maitland afterwards found it difficult to distinguish them in his mind without reference to his notes.

Perhaps it was because in both cases their mothers twittered anxiously over the idea of an interview, and even when Chris had done his persuasive best to convince them of its necessity insisted on being present. Antony found this inhibiting, and without the questions which he might otherwise have pressed more strongly neither of them had anything of moment to add to what he already knew. Simon was the one who had been eager to be friendly, Mark had gone along with him more or less under protest; both had agreed, after the second or third conversational gambit had been firmly squashed, that Tommy wasn't worth any further trouble.

John Thorpe's mother, on the other hand, took their advent philosophically, and left them together with her offspring after admonishing him to tell the gentlemen what they wanted to know, and not any of his fancy stories. Maitland sorted through the contents of his pockets until he found an old envelope that wasn't already written on, borrowed Chris's propelling pencil, and looked hopefully at their witness.

The boy submitted him to a scrutiny every bit as searching, but evidently he passed inspection because after a moment John said in quite a friendly way, 'I wouldn't mind being a barrister myself.'

'Are you interested in the law then?'

'Sort of. I've been getting famous trials out of the library ever since Tommy was arrested. Will he be cross-examined in court? I wish I could be there.'

'As things look at present, I don't expect we shall be calling on him to give evidence.'

'Doesn't he have to?'

'Not necessarily.'

'What a sell.' He brooded about this for a moment. 'I thought he'd get up and say, I didn't do it. And then the—the prosecuting counsel would get after him and he'd break down and confess.'

'It might not work out like that, you know,' said Maitland seriously. 'You wouldn't want him to confess if he were innocent.'

'No, of course not. I say, do you think he's falsely accused.' Luckily, he didn't wait for an answer to that. 'And you're going to clear his name,' he said admiringly. Clearly he had been reading something besides famous trials. 'Will it be by a stroke of forensic brilliance, or will you just find evidence that proves he's innocent?'

Antony smiled at him. 'I'm afraid I can't discuss our case, even with you, John.'

'No, I suppose not.' He heaved a sigh, but he did not seem unduly cast down. 'Will you be calling me then? That would be something, that would.'

'I don't even know yet what your evidence will be.'

'No, I suppose ... I don't know anything, not really. Unless you could use me as a character witness, you know. I thought Tommy seemed a good sort of chap.'

'Was that why you tried to talk to him?'

'Yes, it was. Mark wasn't keen; he didn't say so but I think he thought Tommy looked pretty scruffy. As if it matters what people wear. And I must say Tommy was cagey. He didn't seem to like answering questions, always had some excuse why he couldn't stay and talk.'

'What sort of excuses?'

'He had errands to do, he worked for Mr Curzon, you know. Or he had to get home. Well, I daresay that was true. Old Neale was a queer stick. None of us liked going round that way much.'

'Why not?'

'Oh, he'd wave his stick at you, and shout. Not that I was afraid of him, of course, but there's no sense in stirring up trouble, is there?'

'No sense at all. Did you ever wonder why he behaved like that?'

'Not really. He just didn't like kids, I reckon.'

'Yet he had Tommy living with him.'

'That was different. He was his grandson, wasn't he?' Again he went on without waiting for a reply, for which Antony was duly thankful. 'That's what Mum said, anyway. I wouldn't have cared for living with old Neale myself, but the hut might have been fun. Like camping out.'

'Did you know that Tommy wasn't attending school?'

'Well, I wondered.'

'Why was that?'

'I go to the Grammar School myself, so I know he didn't go there. But I think he was too bright for the Modern School, and as for St Blaise's, old Neale would have died rather than send him among the R.C.s. I mean, they went to chapel *twice* on Sundays, and the Levellers are frightfully hell-fire, you know. I sneaked into one of their services one day, and the preacher wasn't half laying down the law.

But someone spotted me and threw me out before it got really interesting.'

'Did you confide your suspicions to anyone else?'

'My—oh, you mean about Tommy. No, it was his business, wasn't it? Besides, I know I'd be only too glad if I could get out of class occasionally.'

'It might have affected his whole future,' said Conway censoriously. Antony's first reaction to the interruption was one of annoyance, but it gave way to amusement as he watched John grapple with the idea and then dismiss it.

'Even so, it would be up to him, wouldn't it?'

'You talked to him several times, didn't you?' said Maitland hastily, in case Chris took it into his head to point out that thirteen wasn't an age at which one could expect much freedom of choice. 'Do you mind telling us what you talked about?'

'Well, I will, but it isn't really interesting,' said John. 'Besides, if you really want to know, I should have thought Tommy could have told you himself.'

'Have you ever heard of corroborative evidence?' said Antony, rather less than honestly. However, the boy considered this, nodded as if it seemed reasonable to him, and set himself to answer.

'Well, the first time—the three of us were together, you know, Mark, and Sim, and me—the first time he had a basket of groceries, so I wasn't much surprised that he didn't want to stop. Sim said, "Hallo", and "What's your name?" and he said, "Tommy". And then he said, "I can't stop, Mrs Lister's waiting for these", and off he went.'

'Didn't that strike you as a bit unfriendly?'

'Not really. Not then. The next time we saw him was on a Sunday afternoon, quite soon after dinner. He was walking along the track towards Moorfields, quite slowly, kicking up pebbles from the path as he went. And we said, "Hallo", and Sim said, "We're going swimming, do you want to come with us?" and he said, "I can't, I haven't anything to wear," and I told him that didn't matter if we went to our special place, because it was quite private. Then he said, "No. No, I have to get back," and he turned and went back the way he'd come. Only he wasn't in any hurry when we saw him first.'

'What did you think about that?'

'I don't know. Mark thought he was stuck up, and even Sim said we'd better leave him alone, if that was what he wanted. But I didn't say anything because I thought—but is sounds silly to say so—I thought he was plain scared.'

'Of the three of you?'

'I said it sounds silly.'

'So that was the last of your encounters?'

'The last time the three of us tried to talk to him. We'd just say, "Hallo", when we saw him, and go on with what we were doing. But once or twice I thought he looked sort of wistful, as if he'd like to join us after all; and, I don't know, somehow I felt sorry for him—'

'Just a minute, John. Why did you feel that way, do you know?'

'I think I thought he was lonely. After all, it must have been pretty dreary, with only old Neale for company.'

'I see. Go on.'

'It isn't really much, you know.'

'Never mind that.'

'Well, it was about a week before the murder. A little more than a week, because it was a Sunday. I went up to Moorfields on my own after tea, and there was Tommy, chucking stones into the Big Pond. So I sat down and watched him for a bit, and after a while—I think it was because I didn't ask him any questions—he came and sat down beside me and asked me if I'd always lived in Arkenshaw, and how I liked it, and which school I went to, and—oh, a lot of other things. And finally he asked me

54

what I was going to do when I left school, and I said I was going to be a doctor; that was before I made up my mind about the law, you know, and as a matter of fact I don't think we can afford either of them, I shall probably end up in the office at Comstock's Mill, or something dull like that. And Tommy said, "I want to be a sailor", and he sounded sort of—sort of dedicated about it, if you know what I mean. So I asked him a question then, did he mean the Navy? And he said no, the Merchant Service, and I said, Why didn't he run away to sea if he wasn't happy?'

'Had he told you he wasn't?'

'No, but it was pretty obvious really. For a moment I wished I hadn't said anything, because I thought I might have scared him off again. But then he said, "People don't do that now, nobody would give you a berth" which was all very well if he hadn't added, "You'll understand when you're older," which was pretty good cheek, but I didn't say anything. And he talked for a bit about seeing foreign places, things like that, I don't remember exactly, until I put my foot in it again by saying something silly like, "And having a wife in every port", and then he just froze up on me.'

'You mean he didn't say anything more?'

'Only, "Women!", sort of as if he hated them. After a bit we walked back together, but he didn't talk at all, except to say that it was too late now for him to go to chapel. And I didn't see him again after that, only in the distance.'

'I see. Well, that's been very helpful, John, and I'm grateful to you.'

'Will you be ... needing me?' asked John hopefully.

'I don't think so. If we change our minds we'll be in touch with your parents.'

'I just thought ... they won't let me stay away from school to go to the trial, you see. Even though I told them it would be good experience for me.'

'If it's any consolation, you wouldn't see much of it even if you were called as a witness. Not until after your evidence had been given. You'd be cooped up in a waiting room with the other witnesses ... very dull.'

'I still think ... when did you first see a trial in court, Mr Maitland?'

'When I wasn't much older than you are.'

'There, you see.'

'But it was during the school holidays.'

'Oh ... well. Tell Tommy I wish him luck, will you? I wonder why he did it.'

But neither Maitland nor Conway was to be drawn into speculation. They renewed their thanks and left, after a word with Mrs Thorpe, who came out of the kitchen with floury hands to see them go.

VI

Even with so scant a harvest, the three interviews had taken time. Antony suggested a drink at the hotel, but Chris was anxious to get home for a while, before they visited the Reverend Samuel Harte later in the evening. So Antony went back to the Midland Hotel alone, and ordered a drink in the lounge—whisky, because he felt he needed it—and set himself to study the evening paper.

The headlines concerned a proposal by the North Vietnamese negotiators in Paris that the United States should have private and direct talks with the Viet Cong; not very interesting, nothing was going to come of it anyway. He found a discreet reference in the bottom left hand corner of the front page to the fact that Mr Justice Gilmour's list had reached a point where it was almost certain that the trial of Tommy Smith (13) for the murder of Alfred Neale (70) would start on the morrow. Except for a Stop Press item concerning a bank robbery, the back page was entirely devoted to Obituaries, headed by the rather lengthy one of a certain Joseph Taylor, who had been in the employ of Messrs, Henry Spencer & Sons, *Lithographers and photo-engravers* for the last ten years, and who had died after a lengthy illness. Inside, there was sports news, and letters to Aunt Ethel, and tomorrow's horoscopes. Thinking of Grandma, he read his idly. *Travel indicated* (a bit late for that, surely); *take care; there may be conflict with a person born under Pisces.* For a moment he allowed himself to be amused by the possible aptness of that. Chris Conway was a Pisces, as he knew from old Mrs Duckett's frequent grumbling references to the fact. But in spite of her occasional attempts to scare him with sinister prognostications she wouldn't approve, he knew instinctively, of the vagueness of the newspaper's predictions. So he laid the paper aside and concentrated instead on his drink, and on trying to decide the occupation of the stout man sitting near the window, and wondering whether his thin wife was of as sour a disposition as she looked.

Later, he arranged for his apologies to be conveyed to the President of the Bar Mess and ate early in the main dining-room. Chris called for him at eight-thirty, and found Maitland already on the steps of the hotel. They took again the road that was becoming familiar, in the direction of the Town Allotments.

The chapel which the Levellers attended in Arkenshaw was an ugly stone building, which had probably started its life as a small warehouse. It looked to be unnecessarily lofty, just as the cottage beside it, which now did duty as the minister's house, gave the impression from outside that all the ceilings would be too low to accommodate a tall man in comfort.

The Reverend Samuel Harte must have been waiting for their knock, he let them in without any delay at all. He was a tall, portly man, with a shock of grey hair and an excellently tailored suit. The room into which he led them was also furnished, as a study, more elegantly than the exterior of the cottage would have suggested. The desk under the window was highly polished and almost clear of papers, there was a bookcase on the opposite wall that was filled to overflowing, and three leather covered easy chairs arranged rather too neatly around the fire that burned in the old-fashioned grate. There was a moment's skirmishing until they were all seated, and even then Harte was up again in an instant, saying in his deep, pleasant voice, 'At this time of day, a drink would surely not come amiss.'

Whatever Maitland had been expecting it had been nothing like this. Something after the manner of John Knox in one of his more strait-laced moods, most likely. He accepted the invitation now without hesitation, caught Chris's eye for a moment and then looked resolutely away. Conway was obviously as bewildered as he felt himself, but not doing such a good job of hiding it. There was a silence, broken only by the clinking of glass, and presently the hiss of a soda siphon. It was difficult to equate this pleasant room with Alfred Neale and the meagre comfort of the nissen hut; for instance, where did the levelling come in? But Antony was prepared to enjoy himself; it was always gratifying to come across the unexpected.

When they had all been served generously, and Harte was back in his chair again, they discussed idly the weather, and the latest wage claim from the engineering industry, which the minister, perhaps predictably, supported. But it wasn't long before he was saying, in tones which Maitland recognised as gently chiding, 'This is all very pleasant, but I take it your visit concerns my unfortunate disciple, Alfred Neale.'

'And his almost equally unfortunate protégé, Tommy. Who is, as you know, our client,' Antony told him.

'It seems an odd business. I should have thought the Juvenile Court—'

'Not in a case of murder,' said Chris. 'Of course, the court will be kind to him.'

'That won't prevent them putting him in prison if they find him guilty,' Maitland pointed out. 'And the trouble is in these cases finding somewhere to stow the poor little devils away.'

'You think then,' said Harte slowly, 'that the court will find against him.'

'Not if I can help it,' said Antony, smiling.

'You believe his story .... whatever it is.'

'I didn't say that.' No need to explain that the boy had refused to tell a story of any kind ... just a string of denials that might or might not be true. 'But you see, Mr Harte, you must be one of the few people who know anything about the pair of them, beyond the obvious facts that anybody could see for themselves.'

'If you're looking for information, I don't think I shall be able to help you much. I'll try, of course,' he added in a hasty way, as though unwilling to discourage his visitors over much.

'Let's start with Tommy. How long has he been attending your chapel?'

'About three months, at the time of his arrest.'

'From June, then?'

'That's right. I've been to see him in the Remand Home, of course, but I must admit I don't think he found my visit particularly consoling.'

'Did he ... did you have any questions for him?'

'Why, yes. I think that was natural.' He paused a moment, and then went on ruefully, 'Perhaps he thought it was none of my business what he had done; in any case,

I can't say I found him particularly responsive.'

'Did he deny the killing?'

'Yes, he did.'

'And do you think, from your previous knowledge of him, that he was telling the truth?'

'Naturally, I hope that he was. But I think—perhaps I shouldn't say this, Mr Maitland, but unless I am frank with you there is little point in our talking together—I think he was not altogether a willing convert to our views.'

'Neale insisted on his coming to chapel?'

'Yes, I am sure of that. He was in quite a taking, almost the last time I saw him, because the boy had disappeared just when they ought to have been leaving home to attend the evening service.'

'When he did get home he got a beating. Did you know that?'

'No, but ... on the whole I'm not surprised.'

Maitland glanced at his colleague. 'That's what we were afraid of,' he said.

'I don't quite see—'

'If I asked you in court what Neale's reaction would be to so serious a sin as stealing, what would your answer be?'

'He would have punished the boy. Yes, I think so.'

'Severely?'

'If he beat him for missing chapel—'

'Yes, I see what you mean. You don't consider that one of the deadly sins, then?'

'In a boy Tommy's age ... I hoped, as Neale did, that in time he would have become a more willing member of our congregation.'

'I see. You must have talked to him on occasion. What impression did he make on you?'

'A bright boy. Very reserved.'

'And his attitude towards Neale?'

'Respectful. I thought there was some gratitude there, but no affection.' (There was no doubting Harte's intelligence; probably that opinion was as good as another.)

'And Neale's attitude towards Tommy?' Maitland asked.

'That's more difficult. He said—that evening I mentioned to you, when the boy wasn't present—that Tommy was a brand to be snatched from the burning, and that he would not achieve that by being soft with him.'

'That's rather a terrifying point of view ... don't you think?'

Harte smiled. 'I do, indeed.' He paused, and drank from the glass at his elbow. 'I am aware, Mr Maitland, that I am something of a surprise to you. You expected something more in the nature of an Old Testament prophet, did you not?'

'Well—' said Antony. And glanced again at Conway, as though for support. 'I didn't ... I don't ... know much about the Levellers, I'm afraid.'

'Our views are strict, I must admit that. Stricter, perhaps, than is popular nowadays. We believe in sin.'

'And in penance?'

'Certainly, but this has no virtue unless it is self-imposed. It is a matter between each individual and his maker.'

'Then strictly speaking Neale should have pointed out to Tommy the error of his ways, and then left him alone.'

'I think in the case of a boy that age ... the formation of good habits is very important, you know.'

'Even when the subject is unwilling.'

'I should not have said myself that Tommy had reached years of discretion.'

Antony pondered that for a moment. The temptation to argue was strong, because if ever a boy knew how to be discreet ... 'Perhaps you knew Neale better than you knew his ward,' he said at last.

'Certainly I did.'

'When did he first attend your chapel?'

'I have been looking up our records. It is nearly seven years ago now that he first came to the Sunday services.'

'Had he been a member of the sect before that, do you know?'

'I think not. He approached me as a neophyte.'

'I don't know if it's in order to ask you if he spoke to you about himself.'

'We don't encourage confession, you know. A man's own consciousness of his sins is sufficient for forgiveness ... provided, of course, that he is sincere and shows his sincerity.'

'In what way could he do that?'

'By ... well, by modifying his way of life, for instance.'

'Do you think that was what Neale was doing?'

'I think perhaps it had something to do with his choice of habitation. He told me at the first meeting that he was in search of salvation, and asked me whether I could show him the way.'

'And could you?'

'I hope I was able to help him.' That was still said amiably, but something in his tone warned Maitland that he was treading on dangerous ground. He produced his next question with a diffidence that was not altogether assumed.

'May I ask you ... I may be getting the wrong impression? But do you think there was something in Neale's past life that he repented of?'

'I think that is true of all of us.'

'Something specific though?' Maitland insisted.

'He never gave me his confidence, nor did I ask for it. It was sufficient that he became a devout worshipper.'

'But didn't he tell you *anything* about his past life?'

'He had lived in London. He said it was a godless place.'

'Where abouts in London?' It was too much to hope, of

62

course, that they were going to get an address, so he wasn't really disappointed when the minister shook his head.

'That, I am afraid, he never told me.'

'Did he ever mention any relatives?'

'A sister, who died two or three years ago. And a niece is living somewhere in the south, but I did not gather that he was in touch with her.'

'Perhaps he disapproved of her, too.'

'I think you may be right. Contact with unbelievers can be a dangerous thing, you know.'

'You're not afraid to risk it yourself,' said Maitland. Chris, watching him, felt a moment's surprise that he seemed to be perfectly serious. Harte too, was unsmiling as he answered.

'The laws of hospitality are sacred.'

'Thank you.' He did smile then, and picked up his glass for the first time and drank from it. 'I suppose it would be too much to hope that Neale told you where Tommy came from.'

'He did not. The question didn't arise really, I more or less took it for granted that he was his sister's grandson, because Neale had told me once that he had never been married. But cannot Tommy tell you about this himself?'

'He is, as you said, strangely reticent.'

This time it was Harte's turn to say, 'I see,' but he sounded doubtful about it. 'May I ask,' he added, after a short, rather uneasy silence, 'whether this interview is a prelude to my being called as a witness?'

'I think not.'

'I should be glad, of course, if I could help that unfortunate boy.'

'It doesn't sound, really, as if you could give him a very good character reference from your own point of view.'

'If Alfred was right—' He did not attempt to finish the sentence, but shrugged instead and added with an appear-

63

ance of candour, 'I cannot help being glad that you will not need to call me.'

VII

'And what did you think of that?' Maitland asked when they were outside again and walking towards the car.

'He wasn't ... quite what I had expected,' said Conway carefully.

'A hypocrite, would you say?'

''appen,' said Chris, employing, as he rarely did, one of Arkenshaw's favourite words. And then, still doubtfully, 'Yes, I suppose so.'

'A queer chap to find running what you described to me as a hell-fire religion. Perhaps he's different when he gets into the pulpit. And I suppose if each person prescribes his own penances, and he is conscious of his own virtue ... that might explain it, don't you think?'

'I expect you're right,' said Chris slowly. 'He wasn't much help to us, was he?'

'No, but then I didn't think he would be. I wonder if Neale "got religion" at the time he came to Arkenshaw and joined the Levellers, or if he was similarly affected before.'

'If he came from London, I don't believe the Levellers operate there.'

'That needn't have deterred him. He'd have had a dozen equally dotty religions to choose from.' They reached the car then, and he hesitated with his hand on the door. 'However, if Neale really told Harte he was in search of salvation, the idea had most likely just occurred to him.'

'I don't see why Harte should have lied about that.'

'Nor do I.' He pulled open the door and got in. 'Only it

does make me wonder what sort of a life Neale had been living before that, you know.'

Chris let out the hand brake, and shot his companion a startled look before turning his attention to his driving. 'You're theorising ahead of your data,' he said mildly as he pulled away from the kerb.

'Whose fault is that?' Maitland leaned back and stretched out his legs as comfortably as he could. 'If my brief weren't a barren waste, with no inspiration to be derived from it at all—'

'Well, I'm sorry about that, but I did warn you,' said Conway seriously. 'Have you any plans for tomorrow before we have to be in court?'

'Only to find a book shop. If Tommy is keen on the sea, that suggests another course of reading for him, doesn't it? He'll need something to keep him amused over the weekend, and Sir Walter Scott won't last for ever.'

'I'll call for you at a quarter to ten, then. We pass W. H. Smith's on the way to the court,' said Chris. After that they drove in silence until they reached the Midland Hotel, each occupied with his own thoughts.

VIII

Once Maitland was inside the lobby there was a problem to be solved. It was still comparatively early, time to join the Bar Mess for coffee and a brandy, but somehow he didn't want to do that. As he crossed to the desk to collect his key the feeling identified itself more clearly . . . Anderson would be there. He told himself he was being absurdly sensitive, but that didn't help at all. It wouldn't have mattered—at least, he didn't think it would—if he had had the faintest idea of what he was going to say when he got into court. As it was, the thought of the trial made him edgy. Strictly speaking, it needn't worry him until Monday at the earliest, but if he was going to cross-examine the prosecution witnesses with any effect at all, he ought to have some idea of the line the defence was going to take. Sir Nicholas would have told him, no doubt, that a little more cogitation on the subject would not come amiss, but he had lived with it all day and at the moment he felt heartily sick of Tommy and all his works.

However, somehow or other the problem seemed to have decided itself. He had collected the key and was already half way up the stairs. If Jenny hadn't gone to the theatre he would call her and find out what was going on at home, and that might serve—though he wasn't very hopeful—to settle his mind.

Jenny was in, and answered the call on the second ring. 'Are you coming home for the weekend?' she wanted to know.

'As things are at present ... it's a damnable business, love, nothing to take hold of. Nothing I can reasonably do.'

'Then I shall see you,' said Jenny, not trying very hard to disguise the satisfaction in her voice. And then, with a hint of laughter behind what she was saying, 'We can always use Uncle Nick's spare room if the men haven't finished.'

Antony sighed. 'What are you up to *this* time?' he enquired. He sounded resigned, and Jenny laughed outright.

'Nothing much. Only the bedroom did need decorating, and while they were about it I thought I might as well paint the bathroom too.'

'That's all very well, but—'

'Antony, it will all be cleared up by the time you're home for good. You ought to be glad I do these things while you're away, but you're as bad as Uncle Nick, hating disturbances.'

'Haven't I cause?' he asked reasonably. 'I only hope your colour schemes aren't too drastic this time.'

'Well, for the bedroom I chose a rather interesting paper.'

'Exactly what I was afraid of.'

'No, honestly, Antony, I showed it to Uncle Nick and he approved.'

'That's nothing to go by. He'd approve of anything, so long as it didn't interfere with his own comfort. If he'd been haunted through as many sleepless nights as I have—'

'You didn't like the old wallpaper, that's *exactly* why I wanted to change it,' said Jenny triumphantly. 'Anyway, it isn't a bit fair to say that Uncle Nick—'

'He grumbled enough when you had the living-room done.'

'So he did. I almost wish I'd decided to do that again.'

'But it's only a year!'

'Because it might have distracted him.'

'What from?'

'What do you think? Your foolhardiness in going to Arkenshaw.'

'Anyone would think it was the depths of darkest Africa.'

'If you would only refrain from setting the whole town by the ears,' said Jenny, in what he recognised as a parody —though not a very good one—of his uncle's tone.

'The town won't even know I'm here ... or only from the papers.'

'That's just what Uncle Nick is afraid of.'

'Then he's being even more tiresome than usual. They're interested in the case, of course, but only incidentally in me.'

'I'll tell him that. It may console him,' said Jenny doubt-fully. But she added more cheerfully when he did not answer her immediately, 'I met Inspector Sykes in Liberty's today.'

'Did you though? What were you doing in Liberty's, anyway?'

'Well, you see, Antony, the bedroom curtains don't exactly match the new wallpaper.'

'I might have known it, I suppose.'

'Well, yes, I do think you might.'

'Don't bankrupt us before I get home, love.'

'You haven't asked me what Inspector Sykes was doing in Liberty's. That's much more interesting than your—your forebodings.'

'No, and come to think of it, what *was* he doing there?' He could recognise a red herring as well as the next man, but at least they had got away from the subject of Uncle Nick, prophesying doom.

'He was buying one of their silk squares for an old aunt's birthday. Mrs Sykes has lumbago—'

'Poor woman.'

'—and couldn't come to town. And it was a good thing I met him, Antony, because I didn't really like the pattern he had picked out, and I don't see why you should be condemned to wearing pastels just because you're an elderly aunt. So I helped him to decide on a better one.'

'Another interesting design, I suppose. Jenny love, do you really think—?'

'There was nothing wrong with either of them, mine was just more cheerful. So then he took me to tea.'

'Where?'

'A little place in a side street. Very cosy.'

'You won't have noticed, but wherever he is, Sykes knows a little place in a side street where he can get tea.'

'Well, this time I was glad of it. You know shopping always makes me thirsty. Besides, he wanted someone to talk to. He told me all his troubles.'

'I don't believe it,' said Antony flatly, and Jenny laughed again.

'Well, perhaps I wasn't being quite exact,' she admitted.
'He told me a little, and I deduced the rest when I got
home and looked at the paper.'

'You can't stop there, love.'

'I didn't mean to. All he said was that things were just
so-so at the Yard at the moment, and then he talked about
the Assistant Commissioner, as though he had something
to do with it. But before that he'd been having a hate
about newspaper reporters, so I thought perhaps they were
really to blame.'

'That sounds very unlike Sykes.'

'Not really. He didn't really tell me anything at all, now
I come to think of it, just that he was feeling gloomy. But
I picked up an *Evening Chronicle* on the way home and
there was an article in it about the crime rate going up—
I suppose that had been in the morning papers too, but
I didn't notice it—and talking about police inactivity
and they might almost say complacency in the face of
it.'

'Was that all the article said?'

'Well, it talked about organised crime, that might mean
anything, mightn't it?'

'And probably does.'

'Then they said that there had been forged $20.00 bills
circulating in America for years, and the Americans say
they're being brought in from England and nothing was
being done by our police to stop them, which was causing
international tension.'

'Hence these tears. If the police have got the politicians
on their backs—'

'That's not all. The murder rate has gone up, and crimes
of violence have increased. I don't wonder poor Inspector
Sykes felt sad.'

'He'll get over it,' said Antony callously. 'Wait till I
tell you my troubles, love.'

'You said there was nothing to take hold of,' Jenny remembered.

'The thing is, you see, the boy won't talk.'

'Do you mean that literally?'

'No, he's perfectly polite, damn it. But he won't say who he is, or where he comes from, or what he was doing in the Claytons' house, or anything at all except that he didn't kill the old man, and didn't steal anything, although it's almost certain that he did.'

'Does that mean it's almost certain he did the murder too?'

'I don't know! I only know the prosecution's case is horribly circumstantial. Even Grandma couldn't help me make up my mind.'

'Oh, have you seen her? How is she, Antony?'

'The same as ever. She sent her love to you, by the way, and told me to tell you it was a bad time for starting new projects.'

'You're making that up.'

'True as I stand here.' He was sitting on the side of the bed, so that wasn't really a lie. 'And I've had a thought, Jenny. The reason Uncle Nick makes such a fuss about my taking out of town cases is because you always start something while I'm away.'

That was good for nearly five minutes of argument. Contrary to expectation, he was feeling decidedly more cheerful by the time he cradled the receiver and began to make his preparations for bed.

I

The case was called at about eleven o'clock the next day, and Anderson finished his opening remarks before the court was adjourned for the luncheon recess. There was nothing in what he said to give the defence any cause for joy; on the contrary, he sounded depressingly confident, and though that was only to be expected as a matter of tactics Maitland knew him well enough to be sure that in this case there was very little acting about it.

The case against Tommy could be put only too succinctly: he had lived with Alfred Neale, who on one occasion at least had given him a beating. On the night of the 23rd to 24th September he had broken into the house of Mr Robert Clayton and stolen three extremely valuable miniatures, hiding them under his mattress. On Thursday evening, the 25th September, Neale had discovered them, accused him of stealing, and come towards him with his stick upraised. Tommy, remembering what had happened on a previous occasion, had caught hold of the stick, as witnessed by his fingerprints, wrested it from the old man's grasp, and proceeded to batter his benefactor to death. That was told at much greater length, of course, but the picture was very clear. Anderson concluded with a plea to the jury—four women and eight men—not to be swayed by the youth of the defendant. 'The court in its wisdom will take care of his future if your verdict should go against him.'

Antony lunched with Chris Conway and John Bushey in a restaurant not far from the town hall, and perhaps it was not to be wondered at that none of them had much to say.

They returned to court on foot, a matter of necessity as traffic had been diverted from the immediate vicinity in deference to Mr Justice Gilmour's known dislike of noise. The courtroom itself had, as ever, a damp feel about it, and unless you were very lucky you sat in a draught and the light was inconveniently placed. On the judge, a pessimist by nature, this generally had an exhilarating effect as fulfilling his worst forebodings, but today he had a glum look about him. He didn't like a trial where the defendant was no more than a child, and he didn't like the leading counsel for the defence, or trust him either; which was unjust, as Maitland had never behaved other than with extreme propriety on the occasions he had appeared before him, giving little excuse for the accusation of unorthodoxy which Gilmour had heard levelled at him from time to time. But it couldn't be denied that there had been publicity on occasion, which could only, the judge felt (and Antony would have agreed with him), be deplored. That very morning the local paper had run a banner headline: TOMMY 'SMITH' TO BE DEFENDED BY MAN WHO NEVER LOSES A CASE, which, fortunately for his peace of mind, Maitland had not seen. The inaccuracy of the statement, let alone its absurdity, had never comforted him when he had heard it in the past.

Tommy had been given a seat in the well of the court, in a chair very near the table where Maitland's papers were spread. Maitland himself had not taken up his usual somnolent posture during Anderson's opening speech, but had looked instead at his client who was listening gravely to what was said, but apparently with no more emotion than he would have given to a history lesson at school. Apparently ... but once when he turned his head and his eyes met Antony's there was for a moment a look of blind panic, to be succeeded almost immediately by what was unmistakably an appeal. Which did nothing to make counsel feel any happier about his responsibility in the matter. If only he could make up his mind ...

First, there was evidence of identification given by a neighbour of Neale's who had talked to him on occasion when he—the neighbour—was out exercising his dog, and even joined the old man in the hut once or twice on cold nights for a cup of strong, sweet tea. Yes, he had known Neale as a deeply religious man. The boy had been with him since early June, but no explanation had ever been given for his presence. Certainly Neale would have been horrified if he caught Tommy stealing, and he wouldn't be surprised to know ... But here Maitland made his first and last objection of the day, and was surprised and not much gratified to find that it was upheld.

Then came the medical evidence, a gruesome enough description of the wounds the old man had suffered, and a positive statement that death had taken place between nine and ten o'clock on the evening of the 25th September—the day before Neale's body had been discovered. Several times while the doctor was in the witness box Tommy moved uneasily in his chair. The pretence of dissociation was wearing very thin indeed. And there was nothing to be done about it, no point in trying to discredit the doctor, though the downright nature of his observations invited it. It wouldn't have done any good. Only Maitland could ask, when at length Anderson signified that he had finished with the witness and sat down again with a satisfied thump, 'Do you really think the injuries you have described could have been inflicted by a child?' To which the answer came, without any hesitation at all, 'By a boy of thirteen, tall for his age and armed with a heavy blackthorn stick, yes, I do.' The stick had not yet been put in evidence, but when it was the jury would remember that.

After that, parcelling the medical men neatly together,

came the doctor who had been called in to give Tommy a routine examination, in the course of which he had discovered the welts on the boy's back. 'A severe beating,' he said, and Maitland made no attempt to contradict him. He might be glad enough to quote that opinion himself before they were through. It was at this point that he made up his mind he would see Tommy again on the morrow, even though it meant catching a later train home.

The next thing that happened was that Anderson placed in evidence a whole raft of exhibits. There were witnesses to swear to the accuracy of plans of the hut and maps of its immediate neighbourhood; to attest to the taking of photographs, and the receipt by the police of the anonymous letter that had led to the discovery of Neale's body. There were the miniatures, with yet another policeman to tell where they had been found. And after that still more police witnesses. The man from the forensic laboratory at Wakefield, carefully understating his case, to swear to Neale's blood and hairs on the knobbly end of the stick; the fingerprint expert, whom Maitland remembered vaguely from the last time he had been in Arkenshaw. Nothing much to be done there either, except perhaps, 'You say the fingerprints made at the time of the attack were blurred ... too blurred for identification?'

'That is so.'

'Then you have no reason to suppose that they were made by the defendant ... by Tommy Smith.'

'In view of the other evidence—'

'Forget the other evidence. We are concerned only with yours. When first you examined the blackthorn stick what did you find?'

'The defendant's fingerprints and palm prints quite clearly imposed, right hand above left, almost at the end of the stick. And a blur of prints further up, which might or might not have been his, but which I assumed—'

'I think my learned friend will agree with me that we are not concerned with your assumptions, Mr Farraday. The only unmistakable prints, then, were those at the end of the stick. And they were too clear, if I understand you correctly, to have been made in the act of battering an old man to death.'

'That is so,' said the witness again, not altogether happily. Maitland let him go, and Anderson did not avail himself of the opportunity to re-examine. But the glance he directed at the defence counsel said only too clearly, 'Wait for it!' It was noticeable that he himself had examined even the minor witnesses, leaving his junior—a man called Martin, of no particular distinction, but with a good reputation for having a head for detail—with little to do but take the note.

What he was to wait for wasn't immediately apparent. Mr Curzon, the grocer—a mild-looking little man with a minimum of hair and heavy, thick-lensed glasses—was the next witness, and his evidence was ordinary to the point of dullness. On the 6th June he had put a notice in his shop window, saying that he needed a boy to run errands, and that evening the defendant had presented himself to apply for the job. His clothes were shabby, but he—the witness—had been impressed by his good manners and taken him on with very little hesitation. He had asked him where he lived, of course, but old Mr Neale had been known as a religious man, and if anything the fact that Tommy Smith was living with him was a point in his favour. He had asked whether they were related and was told, 'Sort of,' which made him think there was illegitimacy in the picture somewhere, so he hadn't asked any more questions. He *had* asked Tommy where he went to school and got the reply, 'The Modern School,' and for all he knew even now that might be true. No, the boy had never presented himself for work during school hours. If he'd had any suspicion he was playing truant he'd have spoken to Mr Neale about it himself.

Maitland had just one question to ask him. 'What was the last day on which Tommy presented himself for work?' to which the answer came without hesitation, 'The evening of Tuesday, the 23rd September.' Upon which Antony ejaculated, 'Three days before the murder,' and sat down quickly before Anderson could take exception to the remark as irrelevant.

After that came Robert Clayton, whose appearance caused a stir among the spectators; from which Maitland would have deduced, even without what Grandma had told him, that the Chief Surgeon at St Mark's Hospital was a well-known figure in the town. He was a big man, probably in his early fifties; Antony judged him to be about his own height, but he had heavy shoulders and a general air of sturdiness that made him (counsel thought) more impressive. There was, however, no hint of clumsiness about him; his hands were very noticeable, well-kept and deft in their movements. As to dress, he was impeccably turned out. That, somehow, Antony had expected from his reputation as a collector; a man who took pride in his possessions would surely also take pride in himself.

His evidence did not promise to be much more interesting than that of the grocer. He answered Anderson's questions composedly; first, the personal, qualifying questions, and then those concerning the burglary. It happened that he had been the first person to notice that the french window leading from the drawing-room to the garden had been forced open. That would be at about eight o'clock, he had gone into the room just before breakfast to fetch a copy of *The Scalpel* that he had been reading the night before. The forcing would not have been a difficult task, he admitted, a kitchen knife such as the one he was shown (from Neale's hut) could certainly have done the job. Indeed, he had effected entry with his pocket knife on one occasion when the maid had been away and he and his wife had succeeded in locking themselves out. But this time the forcing had been done carelessly, there were scratches on the paintwork. He had searched the house quickly, but there were no signs of any disorder; a survey of his valuables revealed that only the three Holbein miniatures were missing. Yes, those were his property, the miniatures that the usher was showing him; and he hoped —with a humorous look—that the police, or whoever had them in charge, were taking good care of them. Immediately after the discovery of the missing items he had telephoned the police.

Again, Maitland's cross-examination was very brief. As he came to his feet in a leisurely way he caught sight of Tommy, and what he saw puzzled him for a moment. The boy seemed to have shrunk in upon himself, as a small animal, hiding among the reeds or grasses, thinks to escape attention by keeping very still. It was as though the doctor's evidence had come home to him, as that of the previous witnesses, with its more serious content, had not; as though he realised now, for the first time, the reality of his plight.

But there was no time for that now, he couldn't even catch Tommy's eye. And Robert Clayton was waiting, still courteous, still composed. 'These miniatures, these very valuable miniatures,' Maitland said. 'Where were they kept?'

'In the dining-room, hanging on the wall beside the fireplace.'

'In a house so easily broken into?'

'What is the use of having beautiful things if you hide them away?'

'What, indeed?' He paused a moment, but better make the point in his closing speech, perhaps. 'Mr Clayton, what drew your attention to the fact that the french window had been forced? Was it the scratches you mentioned?'

'No. I was surprised to find the window open. I knew it had been shut the night before, and the maid does not usually go into the drawing-room until my wife and I are at breakfast. So I went across to look, and then I noticed the scratches.'

'I see. Thank you, Mr Clayton. That is all.' He wasn't surprised when Anderson declined to re-examine.

Then it was Superintendent Morrison's turn, and that, of course, was when the going got really sticky. It was his job to gather together the threads of the prosecution's argument and elaborate on them to a greater extent than Anderson had already done in his opening address. Maitland had heard of the Superintendent before, but had never actually encountered him. Now he saw a tall, heavily-built man, with sandy hair receding from a rather bulging forehead and mild blue eyes. Morrison gave his evidence in a tone that was faintly tinged with regret, but he was not in the least doubtful about what he had to say.

He started with the theft of the miniatures. The police had been called to the house of Mr Robert Clayton on the morning of Wednesday, the 24th September. The house had been broken into some time after midnight and three valuable miniatures had been stolen. Fingerprints had been obtained from the french window by which entrance was assumed to have been effected, but they could not at that time be identified. In view of their size, it was wondered whether they might be those of a woman.

Because of the value of the stolen goods, he himself had attended on Mr Clayton to take their description. ('And to assure so important a citizen that everything possible would be done towards their recovery,' said Bushey *sotto voce* and cynically to his leader; but Maitland only smiled absently. He was inclined to like what he saw of Morrison himself,

78

and thought he was handling a distasteful job as well as he knew how.)

'And now,' said Anderson impressively, when the miniatures had again been identified as the ones found under Tommy's mattress, 'we come to the discovery of Alfred Neale's body. What took you to the nissen hut in the first place?' he asked.

'Investigations following the receipt of an anonymous letter at the police station on the morning of Friday, the 26th September. It was passed to me for attention because I had been dealing myself with the burglary that took place at Mr Clayton's house, and this letter purported to have information about it.'

'Do you recognise this letter, Mr Morrison? Exhibit number four, I believe,' said Anderson vaguely. To Antony's annoyance, because he was quite sure the other man knew perfectly well how the exhibits were numbered. 'Perhaps you will read the letter to the court,' Anderson suggested, after the Superintendent had given his assent.

' "If you want to know who took the Holbein miniatures from the Claytons' house on Brinkley Drive, the old man who lives in the nissen hut by the Town Allotments could tell you." Of course,' Morrison continued, handing the paper back to the usher again, 'I had no hopes at that stage that anything would come of it; but the matter was so serious that I felt it warranted my personal attention.'

'So you went to the nissen hut without too much delay.'

'In company with Detective Inspector Thorpe. We arrived at approximately ten o'clock and found the door unlocked —in fact, there did not appear to be a lock available—and hanging ajar. When there was no response to our knocks, and I had called out once or twice, I looked through the open door, and though I could not from where I stood see the deceased's body I could see one of his hands. Its

79

position on the floor made it obvious that further investigation was necessary, and we went in.'

'And found the deceased?'

'And found Alfred Neale's body. It was only too obvious that he was dead.'

'Where was he lying?'

'On the floor with his head about two feet from the opening to the rear section of the hut.'

'Yes, thank you. If you will look at your copy of the plan, my lord, and if the jury will do the same, you will see the position marked with some exactitude.' There was a pause, while this was done. Maitland had studied the plan already. He looked instead at Tommy and saw the boy's right hand clenched tightly into a fist. There was no other clue now as to what his thoughts might be.

'And after that?' said Anderson, when he felt sufficient time had elapsed for the plan to be firmly imprinted on everyone's mind.

'Inspector Thorpe left to telephone for the necessary reinforcements. And while I was waiting for him to return the accused came in. When he saw me he would have left again immediately, but I prevented that, and asked him his name, and what he was doing there, and got no reply. So when my men arrived I sent one of them back to the station with him, so that I could question him later myself, at leisure.'

'Did you not think he might be one of the local boys?'

'No, I wondered immediately if he had been living in the hut with Neale. He looked a complete little tramp ... clothes dirty and rumpled, as if he'd slept in them.'

'Thank you, Mr Morrison. Please continue.'

'Yes, well, by the time I was ready to see the boy again we had found the miniatures concealed under the mattress of one of the beds in the inner section of the hut; and the fingerprints that had been found made it clear that either a woman or a young person had been living in the hut besides Neale, and that the same person had left the only set of identifiable prints on the blackthorn stick. There were no prints at all on the miniatures. The next thing to be done, therefore, was to compare these prints with the ones found at Mr Clayton's house, and then with those of the boy who was waiting to be questioned. There was no doubt that they were all made by the same hands. So then I talked to the defendant again.'

'Alone?' asked the judge, coming to life suddenly. But Morrison was not the man to be put out by a little judicial heckling.

'No, my lord,' he replied. 'I admit I was in a bit of a quandary what to do, as I couldn't find that he belonged to anybody. So finally I compromised by getting a police-woman and also one of the probation officers from the Juvenile Court to sit in on the questioning. Perhaps it would set your lordship's mind at rest if I also tell you that he had not been left alone at the station, and had been provided with tea and sandwiches from the canteen, which I am told he seemed to need.'

'Thank you,' said Mr Justice Gilmour, inclining his head. Maitland thought with sudden amusement that the old boy had got more than he bargained for, but if this were true he showed no sign.

'I cautioned him,' Morrison proceeded, 'and told him he needn't say anything unless he wished. He understood that all right, I couldn't get a word out of him except that his name was Tommy; and then, as I put our various discoveries to him he denied quite frantically that he had killed Neale, *or* stolen the miniatures. The matter was urgent, as there was apparently nowhere for him to go, and in any case I had the feeling that he would probably disappear if we let him go for the time being. So after some consultation and a recapitulation of the evidence, I formally charged him with the murder of Alfred Neale.'

'Did he say anything in reply?'

'Only he repeated, "I didn't". But after that he didn't say a word. Well, we had to keep him in the cells that night, until alternative accommodation could be arranged at the Remand Home; anyway, it was convenient because of the Magistrate's Court next morning.'

'I see. Now, to recapitulate, Mr Morrison—' But it was already growing late, and at this point the judge decided that he had sat long enough for one day, and declared the court adjourned. Maitland was disappointed, or would have been if he hadn't expected some such thing to happen. Now the evidence would be gone over and over on Monday morning, fixing it clearly in the jury's mind; whereas if Morrison's examination in chief had been finished this evening Anderson's points would be that much more likely to be forgotten by the time the court reconvened. He smiled at Tommy and said, 'I'd like to see you again tomorrow morning,' and Tommy gave him a look which he couldn't quite fathom, but brightened at the sight of the small pile of books his counsel had acquired for him. Bushey had already gone, but after the boy had been taken away Antony and Chris made their way together towards the doorway.

'What about your train?' Chris asked.

'I'll have to catch a later one. Tommy didn't enjoy today, you must have seen that.'

'I'm not blind. But I still don't think he'll talk to you.'

Antony shrugged slightly. 'Probably not. But at least we've learned one thing today.'

'Have we?' said Chris sceptically. Maitland turned his head to smile at him.

'Yes, I quite realise you don't feel I've earned my fee today. I could have enraged Anderson by constant objections, but—don't you see?—I wanted the witnesses to have their heads. There might have been something to be learned.'

'You say there was ... one thing.'

'Two things, really. Tommy looked like a little tramp when he got back to the hut that Friday morning to find the police in possession. And when they fed him at the police station he ate as if he was hungry.'

'I don't see what you can make of that.'

'Don't you? It's suggestive, that's all.'

'What of?'

'You did say, didn't you, that Neale had a cleanliness is next to godliness thing?'

'I did, but—'

'Don't you think that's interesting? The matron of the Remand Home burned his clothes, if you remember.'

'Most boys positively prefer to be dirty. All it suggests to me is that Tommy knew Neale was dead and was reverting to type.'

'I never knew such a chap for throwing cold water. There's another thing too. What did you think of the Holbeins?'

'I suppose they really are all that valuable. They didn't look like all that much to me. I know the portraits are beautifully executed, but still ... I suppose I'm really trying to say I haven't got a collector's bug myself.'

'You're saying exactly what I thought you'd say ... exactly what I thought myself. And that being so, do you think it likely that a thirteen-year-old boy would know their value, and choose them to steal out of all the contents of the Claytons' house. You say Clayton is a collector, he must have some more showy items among his things.'

'You're saying somebody put Tommy up to it.'

'Am I? If that had happened it must have been Neale, don't you think? And that doesn't seem likely in view of what the Reverend Mr Harte had to tell us.'

They were out in the open now, descending the long flight of steps that led to the street. Traffic was beginning to move into the area again. 'You're making my head spin,' Conway complained.

'I'm sorry. Just idle thoughts, Chris, nothing to worry about. You remember I asked when Tommy did his last errands for Mr Curzon, the grocer?'

'On the evening of Tuesday, the 23rd September.'

'The night before the burglary. Now, why do you suppose he didn't go to work on Wednesday evening, or Thursday. Presumably he still needed the money ... and come to that, how do you imagine he intended to dispose of the miniatures?'

'I haven't any idea. It's queer, but people *are* queer. You're not forgetting, are you, that his fingerprints were found on the french window, and that the miniatures were hidden under his mattress in the hut?'

'No, I'm not forgetting that,' said Antony, and sighed. 'It's a nice evening, Chris. Do you suppose Grandma will give us soused herrings for supper?'

II

In spite of all her talk of economy, with which Antony was perfectly familiar, Grandma Duckett's suppers were always plentiful. That evening there was a vast stand pie and salad; quite an imaginative salad, as a matter of fact. To say nothing of such delicacies as pound cake and parkin, and masses of home made bread. Grandma was hospitable, Inspector Duckett gruff and friendly, Chris Conway was quite at his ease with them both now, Star sparkled quietly, and the baby slept in his carry-cot as though nothing short of an atom bomb would waken him.

As for Maitland, he found himself relaxing gradually from the tensions of the day.

When they had finished their meal and the table had been cleared, and Star and her husband had retired to the scullery to do the washing-up, the other three grouped themselves around the fire again. The old lady was in her favourite Windsor chair, the Inspector had an easy chair that had seen better days and that fitted him like a glove, and Maitland had his favourite perch on an overstuffed pouffe in the corner nearest the oven. 'Well now,' said Inspector Duckett comfortably, 'did things go the way you wanted them to, today in court?' He was a sturdily built man. There looked to be no more grey in his hair now than when Antony had first met him five years ago, and his moustache was just as undeniably sandy, but his blue eyes had a milder look than on that occasion.

'Not so as you'd notice,' said Maitland regretfully.

'How did your client stand up to it?'

'Very well, on the face of it. Underneath ... he's scared.'

'That might not be such a bad thing,' said Fred Duckett judiciously. 'From what Chris has told me—'

Antony interrupted him there. 'Yes, I'm going to see him again tomorrow, perhaps he may be more willing now to talk. But, don't you see, I'd rather he talked to me because he trusted me than because he's afraid?'

'Humph!' said the Inspector. Grandma shook her head in an admonitory way.

'Just so he talks to you,' she said.

'Yes, I know that's the important thing.'

'Did t' prosecution finish presenting their case?'

'No, nowhere near. There's still the bulk of Superintendent Morrison's evidence to come, and I've a few questions to ask him myself.'

'Did they call Mr Clayton today?'

'Yes, they did. I was saying to Chris, I can't think why

85

a boy of Tommy's age should have picked out the miniatures as being particularly valuable, and as for thinking
he could dispose of them ... I don't see how he meant to
set about doing that.'

'Now, there I don't agree with you.' Fred Duckett had
pulled a pipe out of his pocket and began to fill it slowly,
ramming the tobacco down with sharp jabs of a blunt
forefinger. 'You know nothing about t' lad's background,
after all. He may have been brought up in a regular
thieves' kitchen.'

'That's true, of course.' Maitland spoke hesitantly. 'But
somehow I don't think—'

'Why won't he talk to you then? Tell me that.'

'I think he's running away from something, but what or
why I haven't the faintest idea.'

'Well, and perhaps he was. Suppose he was brought up
to steal, some of these kids are. Then he did something to
offend his father, or whoever t' chap was, and mizzled.'

'Wait a bit, that's a new one on me.'

'Mizzled ... made off ... ran away.'

'Oh, I see. Sorry. Go on.'

'I can't explain how he came to take up with Neale—'

'He said he needed somebody who cared what happened
to him.'

'Well then!' He paused to light his pipe, and Grandma
said into the silence,

'It doesn't explain why Alfred Neale took him in
though.'

'I can tell you that too,' said Antony. 'At least, in a
sort of a way. Neale said Tommy was a brand to be plucked
from the burning.'

'Poor lad,' said Grandma, with feeling. Fred Duckett
snorted his disagreement.

'That just goes to show what I'm saying is good sense.
Sithee, lad,' he said earnestly, emphasising his words with

short, stabbing movements with his pipe, 'Neale was strict with him, and I don't suppose he enjoyed it much. But he didn't know where to go, except back where he came from, and t' miniatures were a—a peace offering, I suppose.'

'That's the best explanation I've heard yet,' said Antony, considering it. 'But it doesn't go any way at all towards disproving the prosecution's case.'

'If t' lad is guilty—'

'As he very well may be. I realise that. I realise too that if he is he'll be better off under restraint of some kind. But what if he's telling the truth when he says he didn't kill Neale, didn't steal the miniatures? You see, he's no family, as far as we can tell. Somebody's got to do some thinking for him.'

'You can't blame yourself for t' way things have fallen out,' said the old lady, much as she had done the day before.

'I can blame myself because I'm throwing my hand in,' said Antony.

'Are you doing that?'

'As good as. Oh, I've a few questions to ask in court on Monday, a few things I can say on Tommy's behalf in my closing speech. But that isn't good enough.'

'Never satisfied, you aren't,' said Grandma in a grumbling tone. But Chris and Star came back into the room then, and it was time to give the baby his bottle, and the talk turned to other things.

On the way back to the hotel Maitland told Chris about the Inspector's theory, and agreed with him, rather glumly, that it was probably correct. But it didn't explain everything that was worrying him, not by a long way.

SATURDAY, October 18th

I

He was expecting Conway to call for him at about nine-
thirty the next morning, but at twenty past Star phoned to
say that Chris had been summoned urgently by his opposite
number, the solicitor who had prepared the briefs for the
prosecution. Antony went back to his room, so as to be
readily on call, and went through the *Courier* systematic-
ally from end to end without being very much the wiser
when he had finished. Then he rang home, to tell Jenny
that it didn't look as if he would make even the late train,
but he would try. After that he prowled round the room
restlessly, spending most of the time staring out of the
window at the traffic in Swinegate. He tried to think
constructively about the problems Monday would bring,
but couldn't fix his mind on the subject; went over again
what he wanted to say to Tommy when Chris finally
turned up, which was all very well but it was what Tommy
answered that mattered; wondered futilely what the prosecution had up their sleeve now; and for some reason
found himself going over in his mind Jenny's account of
her meeting with Chief Inspector Sykes in Liberty's. It
was nearly eleven o'clock when a tap on the door, which
he thought meant the chambermaid was losing patience
with him, heralded Chris's return. He came in, closed the
door carefully behind him, and crossed the room to join
his colleague by the window.

'I'm sorry,' he said, 'to have kept you so long.'

'That's all right.' Maitland didn't attempt to add anything. Conway, he thought, had an odd, dazed look about

88

him, and obviously wanted to talk before they left for the Remand Home.

'Star told you where I'd gone?'

'Yes, she did.'

'It's that idea of yours, Tommy's fingerprints. Well, it was a good idea in a way, because it's certainly brought results. On the other hand—'

'I'm not going to like them ... is that it?' said Antony, when Chris showed no signs of wanting to finish the sentence. 'Sit down and tell me,' he said. 'Or would you like a drink?'

'Thanks, not this early.' He sat down, however, in the room's one easy chair, and Antony moved the few paces from the window that would bring him to the stool in front of the dressing-table.

'It's no good trying to break it to me gently,' he said.

'No, of course. The police have found out where Tommy came from,' Chris told him.

'Come now, that's all to the good surely.'

'Wait till you hear.'

'Well ... where?'

'Carlington. That's on the east coast. A holiday resort in a small way, and quite a busy port.'

'I was there once for a day. Not the most attractive place in the world.'

'No, it isn't.'

'Look here, Chris, it's obvious I made a mistake in asking for this information. Let's admit that and get on with it, shall we?'

'You won't like it,' Chris warned him.

'Never mind that!'

'Tommy's name isn't Smith—'

'We were pretty sure of that anyway.'

'—it's Ridehalgh. He disappeared from the town at the beginning of June—I've got the date written down somewhere, but it doesn't matter for the moment—leaving his mother dead in the one room they shared together.'

Maitland's tone sharpened. 'Don't tell me she'd been battered to death too.'

'No. No, she hadn't, but it was murder just the same. She'd been strangled.'

II

There was a long pause. 'I see,' said Antony at length, thoughtfully. 'Is that to be laid at Tommy's door too?'

'The thing is, why did he run away if he didn't do it?'

'Could he—?'

'Easily. She wasn't a big woman apparently, and a blind cord had been used, a sort of garotte.'

'Versatile youngster, isn't he?'

'Antony, it all fits in. A pattern of violence.'

'Oh, yes. Very pretty. You'd better tell me the rest of it, Chris.'

'The prosecution are going to introduce evidence … that's what they wanted to tell me.'

'We can object to that.'

'Yes, but without a hope of success. Evidence of identification, when the whole town, including the judge, are dying to know who Tommy really is. The evidence about what happened to his mother will be purely incidental, to explain how the police had his prints, and Anderson will be careful to point out to the jury that it has no direct bearing on the present case, but I don't see how we can avoid it being given.'

'I expect you're right. Anyway, that wasn't what I meant.' But before Conway could answer that he went on ruefully, 'I've made a mess of things, haven't I? And I thought the position was bad enough before.'

'Don't you think it's better to know?'

Antony smiled faintly. 'That's the commonsense view, certainly. I don't feel quite equal to it yet. Tell me about Tommy and his mother, Chris. You were long enough, they must have briefed you pretty thoroughly.'

'They did.'

'What about other relatives? Hasn't he a father, for instance?'

'Nobody at all, so far as anyone knows. His mother—'

'Hadn't she a name?'

'Nellie Ridehalgh. She was a prostitute.'

'I see,' said Maitland again. 'Not a very high class one, apparently, if they lived in one room.'

'That seems to be about it. An attractive girl, not so attractive as she grew older. The one room had a tiny kitchen, no more than a cupboard really, and they shared the bath and lavatory with the other tenants. Neighbours say Tommy used to keep the room clean and do whatever shopping there was to be done. Nellie never lifted a finger.'

'How did they manage? Circumstances must have made it difficult for her to carry on her profession.'

'Tommy went to the Grammar School. A clever boy, as you surmised. Passed his Eleven-plus with no difficulty at all. In the evenings he used to do his homework in the County Library, and stay there reading until they closed at nine o'clock. After that he'd be around the streets until one or two in the morning; it's a wonder he didn't get into trouble, but somehow he kept out of it.'

'That's not much consolation.'

'I agree with you there.'

Maitland got up and went back to the window. 'What is known about the mother, Chris?' he said, apparently intent on what was going on in the street outside. 'Are they sure—?'

'If they weren't before, they will be now. It would be the hell of a coincidence—'

'Coincidences happen.'

'Yes, but ... I don't think one happened here.' Conway sounded dogged. 'And I think you'll agree with me if you think about it honestly for a moment.'

'Honestly, Chris?' He turned from the window as he spoke, but there was an undercurrent of amusement in his tone.

'Forget for a moment that you blame yourself for bringing the matter to light,' said Chris steadily.

'I see.' He paused, perhaps to attempt to comply with this suggestion. 'You haven't told me yet what's known about the mother,' he said then, non-committally.

'Nothing much. It was a Thursday evening, wet and cold for June. One of the neighbours saw Tommy sitting on the stairs leading up to the second floor at about eleven-thirty.'

'Wait a bit. Which floor was this one room of Nellie's on?'

'Didn't I tell you that? The first floor, at the front. After that nothing is known of what happened until the next day, when the same neighbour went downstairs to borrow some bread—it was still raining, and she didn't fancy a walk to the shops—and went in and found her.'

'Wasn't the door locked?'

'Closed, but not locked. Nellie was lying on the bed, strangled ... well, I told you that. The couch where Tommy used to sleep hadn't been made up for the night. There was a mass of fingerprints, not unnaturally—'

'Any on ... whatever was used as a lever?'

'No. It was a pencil, but there was nothing identifiable. Tommy's prints were all over the place, but they identified them pretty certainly from his schoolbooks. There were some questions asked about Nellie's clients, of course, but

92

mostly they were casuals and nobody seemed to know too much about them. Tommy could have been more inform- ative, very likely, but he had disappeared.'

'So they took it for granted ... didn't they issue a des- cription of the boy?'

'It was in the *Police Gazette* at the time, but nobody in the force here had heard of Tommy then. And by the time he did come to their notice nobody connected him with the story from Carlington. Why should they? They just thought a grand-nephew of Neale's had come to stay with him.'

'Which reminds me, you'd better call your bloodhounds off the search for Neale's sister and her descendants. It's good of you not to say, "I told you so", Chris,' he added, 'but the fact remains that it's my fault they connect Tommy with Carlington now.'

'You said yourself he'd be better under restraint of some kind.'

'*If* he was guilty.'

'You mean you still don't think—'

'I'm being unreasonable, I know. I'm sorry. But don't you think we ought to hear what Tommy has to say?'

'If anything. He hasn't been exactly loquacious so far.'

'This might make a difference ... don't you think?'

'If you really want my opinion, no.' Conway sounded discontented, but he got up as he spoke. 'We're later than we said we'd be already, but I suppose we may as well find out which of us is right.'

III

Tommy was reading when they went into the deliberately cheerful room. On second sight Antony decided that this was as bad as prison visiting, if not worse; bright curtains and upholstery couldn't disguise the fact that the door was locked, and that when they weren't there a warder was continually with the prisoner. The boy looked up as they went in, and laid his book, open, on the table. 'I thought perhaps you'd changed your mind about coming,' he said.

The warder got up and went out with a muttered greeting. Chris said, 'Something came up, we couldn't get here any sooner,' and looked a little helplessly in Antony's direction. Antony seated himself near the table and asked casually, 'How are the books?'

'They're splendid!' Tommy spoke emphatically, but he looked nervous. 'You said, "something came up", Mr Conway. Do you mean, something about me?'

'Yes, Tommy, I'm afraid so.' Conway glanced at Maitland again; in the boy's presence he seemed ill-at-ease. 'We know who you are now.'

Tommy said nothing, but Maitland had the impression that he grew smaller under his eyes. After a moment Chris went on, 'I hope that will make a difference. I hope it means you'll be ready to talk to us now.'

'Why should I?' He paused, looking from one of them to the other; as on their previous visit, the blunt question gave no effect of rudeness. 'What else do you know ... besides my name?' he asked.

'We know you came here from Carlington. We know ... about your mother,' said Chris, still hesitantly.

When the boy did not reply to that Maitland took up the questioning gently. 'Did you know that, Tommy ... that she is dead?'

For a moment there was no answer to that either, and then Tommy gave a quick, emphatic nod. But he still did not speak.

After a while Antony went on carefully, 'Can't you see that you'll have to tell us your side of the story now?'

'I don't see what good it can do.'

'If I'm to tell the court anything on your behalf, it has to come from you.' Another pause. 'Did you kill your mother, Tommy?'

'No, of course not. I didn't kill anybody!' said Tommy in a goaded tone.

'I can repeat your denial to the court, but standing alone it won't get us very far.'

'It'll be better than saying, I did it ... won't it?'

'Not necessarily. There might be extenuating circumstances ... do you understand what I mean by that?'

'Yes, I think so.'

'If you admitted the truth of the prosecution's case, and said you were afraid of Neale—'

'They'd still say I'd killed my mother. That's what you think, isn't it? And what excuse could I make for that?'

'You must have had some reason.'

'But I tell you, I didn't!'

'You'd better understand the position, Tommy,' said Conway, breaking a rather tense silence. 'The jury will be told who you are and how your mother died, but they will be carefully instructed that they must not let this fact weigh with them in considering their verdict.'

'That doesn't seem fair.'

'Fair or not, that's how it will be, unless Mr Maitland succeeds in getting the evidence ruled out of court. He'll try to, of course, but neither of us thinks he will succeed. And with the best will in the world to consider the evidence in one case, the jury will be swayed by what they hear. They'll be ready to think you mad, but they'll think you killed both of them. So don't you think you'd better tell us your side of the story?'

This time the silence was a very long one. Conway sat waiting placidly enough, but Maitland was possessed by a sudden urge for movement and kept his place only with difficulty. If Tommy was to reach a decision, nothing must be allowed to distract him, but he was still afraid ...

'I suppose I must,' said Tommy grudgingly. 'But I don't think it will help, you know.'

'Let us be the judge of that,' said Chris, just as though he hadn't won an unexpected victory. Antony leaned forward, carefully concealing his eagerness.

'Start with your life in Carlington,' he said, but added cautiously, a moment later, 'And if you say again, "it won't help", I shall probably lose my temper.'

'When I was little we had two rooms and our own bathroom,' said Tommy, not apparently much perturbed by this threat. 'Things weren't so bad then,' he added, looking back on Utopia. 'Then about three years ago we moved into one room. Mother said it would be less work, but I don't think that was the reason. It was awkward then, because there'd be times when I had to be out. There were always ... men. Do you know about that too?'

'Don't worry, Tommy. We understand that part.'

'Yes, well, I don't suppose it was her fault really,' said Tommy thoughtfully. 'I think it was the only way she knew of making a living. It *was* awkward, but I got things worked out fairly well. I'd go home and change after school; it took some doing, raising the money for clothes, so I had to be jolly careful. Then I'd get us both something to eat, and go round to the library to do my homework, and I could read there until they closed.' (And that, said Maitland to himself, with some satisfaction, as at a puzzle solved, is where the boy gets his undeniably fine vocabulary.) 'Later on,' Tommy was saying, 'mother used to leave a chink in the curtains if it was all clear, or if it was wet I'd sit on the stairs going up to the next floor, and go in when I saw somebody leave. That's what I was doing the night she was killed.'

'Tell us about that, Tommy.'

'There's nothing to tell really. There was a man there,

96

and he went and I went in, and she was dead. So I went away.'

'But didn't you realise—? Couldn't you have identified the man for the police?'

'Well ... yes, I could.' That came out reluctantly. He wasn't looking at Maitland now.

'Then why on earth ... did you think you'd be suspected?'

'No, honestly, it never occurred to me until Mr Neale wouldn't believe what I told him.' He raised his eyes again, suddenly eager to have his story credited. 'Then, of course, I realised what a mess I'd made of things by running away.'

'Look here, Tommy, you can't leave it there. If you didn't think you'd be suspected, why didn't you run out and find the nearest neighbour when you found your mother dead?'

'Because ... oh, because I liked *him*, you see.'

'The man who murdered your mother?'

'Well, he must have done. She was certainly alive earlier in the evening, and I'd been sitting on the stairs for nearly an hour. I don't think he'd have stayed that long if he'd found her dead, would he?'

'I shouldn't think so.' He turned to Conway as he spoke, and said rather wildly, 'Good heavens, Chris, did you ever hear the like of it?'

'Never,' said Chris, rather grimly, his eyes on Tommy's face. And then, 'Who was this man you say killed your mother?' he asked.

'He ... he was a sailor.'

'I think I'm beginning to see,' said Maitland, but he said it without any jubilation. 'Didn't you love your mother, Tommy?'

'No, I didn't. I know I ought to be grateful to her, she did the best she could to find me money for the things I needed for school, and I expect that was why we moved into

97

the one room. Only it was lonely, you see, she never seemed to be really interested. Mr Neale said that was another sin, but, honestly, I don't think she wanted me to love her.'

'And this man, this sailor—?'

'He was always decent to me. He'd been coming on and off for nearly two years—he was in the Merchant Service—and if I was there when he came in he'd always make me stay a while, and he'd ask me about school and tell me about what it was like at sea. That's why I thought when I was old enough I'd try for that sort of a job myself.'

'I see. And even what he did didn't change your opinion of him?'

'No. Mr Neale said I was an unnatural son, but ... she used to tease him, Mr Maitland. I'd have been mad if it had been me.'

'All the same, Tommy, I think you're going to have to tell me this man's name, and the ship he serves on.'

'That's just what I don't want to do.'

'I realise that, but don't you realise the position? If the prosecution introduce this evidence and we can refute it, it might incline the jury in your favour on the other charge.' He caught Conway's eye as he spoke and said, 'Don't you think so, Chris?' and Chris replied bluntly.

'I think you're on dangerous ground.'

'Because I ... well, we'll argue about that later. Meanwhile ... you're going to tell us, aren't you, Tommy?'

'I suppose I must. He's called Will Roper, and his ship is the *Red Jacket*. She carries general cargo, mostly on quite short trips to the continent, and she's called after one of the old clipper ships, Will says.'

'Good. Now, tell us what happened after you left Carlington. Did you walk all the way here?'

'Yes. I thought at first about trying to get a lift on a lorry, but then I thought the driver might ask questions, so it wasn't such a good idea. Besides, I wasn't really going anywhere, you see, so it didn't matter how slowly I went. I slept in barns, mostly, and that was a bit tricky because farm work starts so early; but it's surprising how ready people are to feed you if you say you've come farther than you meant from home and are hungry. By the time I'd got to Arkenshaw, though, I was beginning to realise it wasn't a very sensible adventure. So I thought I'd try to get a job running errands, and there might be an empty house I could camp out in, or something like that.'

'How did you meet with Neale?'

'That was how ... looking for somewhere to stay. The nissen hut didn't look occupied ... it was warm weather by then and the stove wasn't lighted. So I pushed the door open, and before I had time to see that someone was living there Mr Neale fairly pounced on me. And he wouldn't believe me when I said I came from not far away; I suppose I was pretty dirty and disreputable by then.' In contrast to his former silence, Tommy was almost gabbling now. 'So he made me tell him all this, but I didn't tell him Will Roper's name, and that was awful because he didn't believe me, and I'd never thought until that moment that perhaps people might not. Then he prayed for guidance, for an awfully long time, and then he said that the Lord had told him that my mother was a worthless harlot, and that he should not give me into the hands of ungodly men, lest they corrupt me even further, but that I must live with him and live so as to expiate my sin. I wasn't absolutely certain what that meant, but I think I learned during the next few weeks, because he was always reminding me. Anyway, after that he started the stove and heated some water and made me wash all over, and he gave me some supper, which I'd have been glad of first, to tell the truth. And after that I stayed with him. It seemed a—a sort of solution, and besides I was afraid if I ran away again he'd tell the police about me. And by then I was frightened for myself as well as for Will.'

He finished up breathlessly. Antony said very quietly, 'You know what I'll have to do now, don't you?'

'I suppose you mean ... find him.'

'There's nothing else to be done. You do see that, don't you?'

'He'll think I'm a traitor.'

'I should imagine he'll think you're a pretty good friend, to have kept silent so long.'

'They won't hang him, will they?'

'Nobody is hanged nowadays. You needn't worry about that.' Conway made a sudden movement, and he turned to look at him. 'Yes, I know what you're thinking, Chris. We'll talk about it later, shall we?' Then he looked back at the boy again. 'Now you're going to tell me—aren't you? —why you went to Mr Clayton's house, and where you'd been the night Alfred Neale was killed.' And again there was the sensation of withdrawal, that Tommy seemed to shrink in upon himself, to look at his counsel warily, from a great distance.

'I don't—' he said huskily, and then started again. 'I'm sorry, Mr Maitland, I don't think I can do that.'

'Why not? It isn't so difficult, you know, once you get started.' Tommy made no reply to that and he added, with a touch of impatience in his voice, 'Don't tell me you're shielding somebody else!'

'No,' said Tommy. His lips were quivering now, and he brushed a hand impatiently across his eyes. 'No, I'm not shielding anybody, Mr Maitland ... only myself.' And he began, helplessly and brokenly, to cry.

IV

Half an hour later they were back in the car again, but Chris made no immediate move to drive away. Instead he twisted in his seat until he could look squarely at his companion, and then said abruptly, 'You'd better tell me what you mean to do.'

'All in good time, Chris. Tell me first, what's biting you?'

'Everything!'

'That's comprehensive enough, certainly. Be a little more specific now.'

'All right! You've given the boy hope where there is none—'

'Not unless he'll talk to me about the second murder.'

'—and you've pledged yourself to try and free him, when you know as well as I do he isn't fit to be at large. That's about enough to be going on with ... don't you think?' This echo of one of Maitland's favourite phrases was thrown out deliberately and savagely. Antony took a moment to reply.

'Now, that's where we differ,' he said at last. 'I happen to believe what Tommy has told us.'

'Antony, you can't!'

'Why not?'

'It isn't reasonable. It isn't ... sane.'

'I'm sorry you should doubt my sanity.'

'Well, look here, even if you do believe him, what about old Neale. He practically admitted that.'

'It didn't strike me that way. He's frightened of something. Couldn't you smell his fear, Chris? He's scared stiff.'

'Afraid of the consequences of what he's done. *That*

doesn't surprise me,' said Chris stubbornly.

'I don't happen to believe he's done anything particularly bad. Though I admit,' he added consideringly, 'I'd be happier if I knew why he broke into the Claytons' house.'

'And so should I! Just because he cried on your shoulder—'

'Yes, that was consoling, wasn't it? But at least I'm not the one he's frightened of.'

'If you're insinuating—'

'Nothing of the kind. Come off it, Chris. We'll get nowhere with this bickering.'

'You've got some idea into your head,' Conway grumbled. 'You'd better tell me what it is.'

'I'm remembering something Grandma told me.'

'For heaven's sake!'

'As for telling you what I think, I don't believe you're ready to hear it yet. If we find Will Roper now—'

'I might have known that was the next item on the agenda.'

'I think you might. That being so, Chris, we will go back to the hotel, or to your office, whichever you like, and you'll phone the Harbour Master at Carlington to find out if the *Red Jacket* is in port.'

'It's a hundred to one chance against.'

'Not so much as that, surely? Tommy said she generally made quite short runs. Anyway, we can but try.'

'And if she is, you'll go to the police, I suppose.' Chris's anger had burned itself out, he sounded now genuinely concerned. 'Isn't that to risk making a fool of yourself,' he asked.

'It might be, but that isn't what I meant. I want to see Will Roper for myself. If he's well disposed towards the boy—'

'You're looking for a confession? What will you do when he tells us he left Nellie alive and well?'

'At least, we've a better chance of getting the truth out of him than the police have ... don't you think?'

'If it is the truth,' said Conway sceptically.

'I'm sorry, Chris, really I am. I know I'm a trial to you,' said Antony, but there was a gleam of amusement in his eye and Chris laughed reluctantly.

'I can see you mean to have your own way,' he said, and slid round in his seat to face the controls again. 'We'll go to the hotel, shall we? Then we can lunch there. Star isn't expecting me.'

'That's a good idea. I can phone Jenny too. How long does it take to get to Carlington?'

'By car? Two and a half hours, if the roads are clear. But don't get your hopes up, Antony, we're not going to find Roper there waiting for us.'

'Something's got to go right sometime.' But the first flush of excitement had faded now, and he spoke with more conviction than he felt.

But for the first time since the case began fortune favoured him, or so it seemed. The *Red Jacket* was in dock at Carlington.

I

They reached Carlington in time for dinner on the Saturday night, and were down at the docks at an early hour the next morning. These were in the old town, which Antony found far more attractive than the new town which he had seen on his previous visit, and which was mainly occupied in catering to the holiday maker.

It was another fine morning, sunny and warm for October, and their luck still seemed to be holding. They found two men by the quayside who had just taken and secured a rope from the incoming *Scarborough Castle*, and who were able to point out the *Red Jacket*'s berth some two hundred yards away. She was a small ship when compared with the others they passed as they walked along, which Antony found encouraging. 'If Will Roper isn't on board there's likely to be someone who knows his address,' he said. 'And if you want to spend the rest of the day tracking down the owners and trying to persuade them to produce a crew list, I don't.' Chris had made no further protest since they started the day before, but he couldn't be called enthusiastic. Now, however, he quickened his pace a little.

Surprisingly, they found the captain himself on board. Perhaps he preferred his quarters there to any accommodation the town had to offer. He was a small man, as trim as his ship. 'Will Roper?' he said in answer to Maitland's question. 'He's my first mate. What do you want with him?'

'A matter he can help us with,' said Antony quickly.

And added, 'We're lawyers,' for good measure, which fortunately proved to be introduction enough.

'You'll find him at number 23 Singer Street. Did you come by car?'

'Yes.'

'Then drive back along Water Street towards the new town. You'll find Singer Street on the left.'

'Thank you. There's one thing more. Were you in port here on the 3rd June?'

That brought a sharp look from the captain. 'I'd have to look it up.'

'Well ... do you mind?'

It seemed he didn't, though he had a doubtful look as he left them to go to his cabin. 'We were, as a matter of fact,' he said when he returned, still with a puzzled look on his face. 'We sailed on the 4th for Rotterdam and Ostend.'

They thanked him again and withdrew in good order. 'But it doesn't prove anything, you know,' said Chris as they walked back towards the car.

'Don't I know it!'

'Have you thought what you're going to say to this chap, Roper? You can't just walk in and say, "I think you killed Nellie Ridehalgh." '

'It may not be necessary to be quite so crude,' said Antony. Chris gave him a suspicious look, but he seemed perfectly serious. 'We shall have to play it by ear,' he said then. 'Or would you rather I saw him alone?'

'Of course not. You may need me,' said Chris firmly, obviously envisaging something in the nature of a brawl. Maitland did smile then, but...

'I'll be discretion itself,' he promised.

Number 23 Singer Street proved to be a little larger than its neighbours, but no more well cared for. A boarding house apparently. PERMANENT AND TRANSIENTS said a crudely printed notice propped up in the front window. Antony used the knocker and hoped for the best.

The door was opened by a tiny, gnome-like woman who was very, very deaf, so that he wondered afterwards how she had heard the knocking. They both roared at her in turn, which elicited finally an offended look and the information that Will Roper's room was on the right at the top of the first flight of stairs, 'but he won't be pleased to see you at *this* hour on a Sunday.' After that she left them to their own devices, so they followed her directions and went up to the first floor.

Truth to tell, Maitland was relishing the coming interview no more than Conway was. Perhaps for this reason his knock on the door of the room on the right was loud and demanding. There was no response at all for a moment, and then bed springs creaked alarmingly, as though a heavy body had heaved itself upright, and a voice, drugged with sleep, demanded huskily, 'Who's 'at?' When there was no response to this query the bed creaked again, and a moment later the door was yanked open. The man inside was large, unkempt and unshaven. 'Hammering on a chap's door in the middle of the night,' he said bitterly.

'I'm sorry we disturbed you. We want to talk to you,' said Antony apologetically. 'If we may come in—'

Surprisingly, the big man made no reply to this, but backed away from the doorway as if this mild speech alarmed him. Maitland went in, and Chris followed him. The room was frowsty, the window tight shut and the bed a tangle of coverings, but it was larger and better furnished than anyone would have guessed from the outside appearance of the house.

'Are you William Roper?' asked Maitland, realising as he spoke that this query should logically have come first. This time he got a reply.

'That's me.' He was overweight, even for a man whose

106

height topped Maitland's by at least two inches, and his face was twisted at the moment into a ferocious scowl, which didn't seem to match his rather mild brown eyes. His hair was a light, sandy colour, so that the fuzz on his chest looked almost golden, and he was wearing the bottom half of a pair of blue cotton pyjamas, tied rather loosely around the waist. 'Who are you anyway?' he demanded, when the silence had lengthened a little.

'My name's Maitland. This is Mr Conway. We're lawyers. If you'd rather dress—'

'Get it over with, now you're here.' He did, however, button on his pyjama jacket, which was lying folded surprisingly neatly on top of his clothes from the day before. When he had done this he tossed the clothes on the bed, sat in the chair, and said, still truculently, 'Sit down if you want to.'

Chris, who so far hadn't spoken, went across to take a chair by the window, turning it so that he could keep an eye, impartially, on both his companions. Antony came far enough into the room to rest his hand on the knob at the foot of the brass bedstead. He said, with the air of diffidence that could be so misleading, 'Have you been in port long?'

'Three days, if you must know.'

'Then you'll have had a chance to see the newspapers.'

'What's that to you?'

'I was wondering whether you'd noticed that the trial for murder of a boy known as Tommy Smith had begun in Arkenshaw.'

'Yes, I saw that.'

'I said, "known as Tommy Smith". His real name is Tommy Ridehalgh.'

'*What?*' Maitland repeated what he had said. 'But ... an old man, it said, the boy had been living with. Tommy lives in Carlington.'

'Up to the 3rd June he did. I assure you it's the same boy, there's no room for doubt.'

'I don't understand.' He shook his head as though trying to clear it. 'They can't do that to Tommy.'

'I'm afraid "they" are doing. We're his lawyers, that's why we're here.'

'I can't help you, mister. I know nowt about it.'

'I don't suppose you do. But if you'll think for a moment—'

'I don't have to talk to you.' He surged to his feet as he spoke. 'Get out!'

Maitland stood his ground. 'Tommy said you'd been kind to him,' he remarked casually.

'What of it?' He still sounded gruff, but he stayed where he was, and his attitude seemed less threatening.

'I didn't think you'd want him to suffer for something he didn't do.'

'I know nowt about this old man.'

'If you remember, I never implied that you did. I'd better explain how we come to be here.'

'Tommy sent you, is that it?'

'Not exactly. We never knew his name until yesterday morning, he refused to say who he was, or where he'd come from. When he was finally identified yesterday it was by his fingerprints, and of course quite a few things came to light, including the fact that he ran away from Carlington the day his mother was murdered.'

'I know nowt of that neither.'

'Don't you, Mr Roper?'

'Tommy's not being tried for that.'

'No, but what happened will almost certainly come out in court, and as certainly prejudice his chances—'

'If he killed this old man he was living with, why shouldn't he suffer for it?'

'The thing is, you see, I don't think he did.'

'It's still nowt to do with me.'

'I think it is. I think you owe something to Tommy for his loyalty to you.'

'What do you mean?'

'That he refused to say who he was because he was afraid he'd have to give evidence about the night of his mother's death. He was afraid he'd have to incriminate you.'

Roper was very still now. Chris thought of the eye of the storm, and his uneasiness grew. Antony was intent on the man he was questioning, and hardly conscious any longer that Conway was in the room. 'I don't have to believe that,' said Will Roper roughly.

'You don't have to, certainly. But if you think back a little, you'll find it's consistent with Tommy's character. And if you imagine it was easy, keeping quiet, you're not thinking straight yourself. He was alone, among strangers, and he was very frightened—'

'Damn you!' said Roper. 'Damn you!'

'—and it was only yesterday that we succeeded in getting him to talk at all. Even then, he didn't want to give us your name, but Mr Conway persuaded him.' He broke off there and Chris, turning for a moment from his scutiny of Will Roper, saw a rather dazed look come into his eyes, as if he had momentarily forgotten where he was. But the impression was gone in a flash, and Antony was continuing earnestly, 'He didn't kill his mother, Mr Roper, and you know it.'

'I went to see her that night, that's true.'

'And were with her for at least an hour, as Tommy can testify. He can also testify that when he went into the room immediately after you left she was dead.'

'But—'

'Nobody will believe him. They'll think he's mad, to have committed two murders, and that seems to be something that Tommy is particularly afraid of. But that's nothing to you, of course.'

Roper was too tanned to go pale, but he was sweating freely now. 'You've got a nerve, haven't you, coming here?' he said hoarsely.

Maitland appeared to consider this. 'I don't think so,' he said at last. 'Tommy obviously thinks a lot of you. I hoped that perhaps you felt the same about him.'

There was another silence, longer this time, but no less uneasy. Finally Antony spoke again. 'You did kill her, didn't you?' he asked quietly.

'What if I say I didn't? You say yourself the police won't believe a word Tommy says.'

'I'm afraid that's true.'

'Then you can get to hell out of here!'

'Very well. And what shall I tell Tommy?'

'Tell him ... God damn you to hell, you know I killed her, don't you? Well, I did, and she deserved it, the lying little whore.'

Maitland, who hadn't been conscious of holding his breath, gave a long sigh. 'That's as good a plea as any ... provocation,' he said. 'Do you want to tell us—?'

'I wanted her ... oh, I know what her life was. I wanted her and I wanted the boy ... a son! Only she'd have to have given up the others. I could have kept them, no difficulty there. Only she laughed at me, said I was a fool ever to have believed she'd change.'

'I see. You'll need a solicitor, Mr Roper, and when you have one you'll have to go into things in much greater detail with him. He'll advise you—'

'Not so fast. What do you want me to do?'

'I want you to come with us to Arkenshaw now, and go to the police there. And I want you to give evidence at Tommy's trial tomorrow, or perhaps Tuesday, for the defence.'

'That's asking something, isn't it?'

'I'm well aware of that.'

'If I say I won't?'

'We shall repeat to the police what Tommy told us, and tell them about this interview.'

'Will they believe you?'

'Oh, I think so. But anything they might do would be too late to help Tommy very much.'

'And if I say I'll go along with this fool idea of yours?'

'Mr Conway and I—and Tommy—will be grateful to you.'

'All right then ... I'll do it.' He paused, ruminating. 'I'll not be too sorry in one way, it's been hanging over me ever since, if you know what I mean. How she looked when she was dead. Haunting me, like. Then you can tell Tommy —can't you?—that I'll see him in court.'

II

Downstairs, standing in the sunshine by the car while Roper dressed and packed his bag, Chris gave voice to his disquiet. 'You've no right to take him out of the jurisdiction of the Carlington police.'

'I daresay not, but I'm going to. He's our surprise witness, Chris, don't you see? And in Arkenshaw he'll be handier to answer our *sub poena.*'

'If the prosecution agree not to mention the fact that Nellie Ridehalgh was murdered—'

'Agree not to ... I shall insist that they mention it. To produce Roper in person will have an altogether dispro-portionate effect to the value of his evidence. And there's still the question of why Tommy left Carlington, isn't there? We can explain that at last, and present him in a sympathetic light to the jury at the same time.'

'That's all very well. You said yourself he'd be better under restraint.'

'And you've been repeating it to me ever since like a gramophone,' said Antony tartly. 'In any case, I only said he'd be better under restraint *if* he killed Neale.'

'And now you've made up your mind that he didn't.'

'I'm afraid I have.'

'Just because you're sorry for him.'

'I can't deny that. He's rather a forlorn character, isn't he? Can you imagine being so starved for affection that a few kind words—'

'Save it for the jury,' said Chris. He was more moved than he cared to say, so he spoke disagreeably.

'Like the infant in Chesterton's poem,' said Antony, ignoring him, 'which I daresay you know now that you've started reading him.'

'Which poem?'

'The one that starts:

I remember my mother, the day that we met,
A thing I shall never entirely forget;
And I toy with the fancy that, young as I am,
I should know her again if we met in a tram.'

'That's not really an exact parallel,' said Chris, as dampingly as ever Sir Nicholas spoke.

'Never mind. It's time I told you what's on my mind, Chris. Will you take me to see Grandma as soon as we get back to Arkenshaw and are free of the police.'

'If you like, but—'

'Then I'll tell you, it will save going over it twice.'

'You can talk as much as you like about the case as it appears in the papers, but you can't discuss *our* strategy with Grandma,' said Chris, horrified.

'Why can't I? She's our—our special consultant,' said

Antony, pleased with the phrase. 'Seriously though, we may want her help. She knows more about Arkenshaw than even you do.'

'Oh, very well,' said Conway, but he sounded faintly huffy now. Perhaps it was as well that the door of the house opened at this point and William Roper came out.

III

They made good time on the return journey, most of the traffic that day being towards the coast, not from it. Antony insisted on stopping for lunch at an hotel in a village not far from Arkenshaw, and over a glass of beer Roper, who had been silent in the car, became talkative; mainly about his relationship with Nellie Ridehalgh, which confidences Chris received in silence, and Maitland with a simple and unaffected interest. It was almost two o'clock when they reached the police station and asked for Superintendent Morrison to be summoned, and turned half past three when they left again. During that time Will Roper's statement had been made and signed, and he had been formally charged with the murder of Nellie Ridehalgh. After he had been taken to the cells, the police in Carlington were informed; there seemed to be some sort of protest going on at the other end of the conversation, but Superintendent Morrison was as firm as even Maitland could have wished in saying that Roper must remain in Arkenshaw to give evidence the next day. The officer most concerned was, of course, there already, as he too would be needed in court.

Outside, Chris heaved a sigh of relief. 'That went off better than I expected,' he said. 'It'll be one in the eye for Anderson all right.'

'So it will.' Maitland set off in a hurry for the spot

where the car was parked. 'It is kind of you not to remind me, Chris, that we've still got the greatest hurdle of all to surmount. We've still no case where the other murder is concerned.'

'You said you had ideas about that,' said Conway, not without a little gentle malice. 'I'm waiting until I've heard them, that's all.' He was unlocking the car as he spoke, and did not go on until they were both settled in their places and the engine was running. 'Old Peel Farm?' he said then, and did not quite hide the disapproval in his tone.

'If you please.' The confident mood seemed to have left him now, he sounded tired and uneasy. 'Tommy was right about his friend, Will Roper, wasn't he? I wonder what will happen when he comes to trial.'

'The fact that he confessed, and the reason for it, will create a favourable atmosphere,' said Conway, negotiating the turn into Cargate. 'If his counsel can persuade the court ... you said yourself, provocation,' he continued, not altogether lucidly. 'I can't say I altogether care for what I've heard of Nellie Ridehalgh myself.'

Antony had a smile for that. If Chris the strait-laced could go so far as that towards condoning murder, there was some hope for Will Roper after all. 'I can't say I've altogether enjoyed the last two days,' he admitted.

'Given what you believed, it was probably your civic duty,' said Chris unsympathetically.

'Surely not. I say, I've only just thought, Chris, what shall we do if Inspector Duckett is in? We can hardly turn him out of his own kitchen, and he'd laugh his head off if I spun some of my theories in front of him.'

'Don't worry about that, he's on duty this week-end. He won't be in until turned six o'clock,' Conway told him. And after that they drove in silence up the long hill.

The house looked mellow in the afternoon sunlight.

There were michaelmas daisies and some chrysanthemums in the garden, and the golf course, completed only last year, made a handsome background. But Antony was in no mood to dwell on the beauties of nature, he took the path up to the front door almost at a run and knocked without looking round to see if Chris was keeping up with him. Old Mrs Duckett opened the door to them with no more delay than was necessitated by the time it took her to get up from her chair, and greeted them without apparent surprise. 'Oh, it's you, is it? Want your tea, I expect,' she said as she led the way to the kitchen. 'Well, you can just fill the kettle, Chris, and get out the cups and some parkin that's in t' tin.'

Chris gave Antony an amused look, and took the big iron kettle into the scullery to fill. Antony waited until Grandma had seated herself again in her favourite Windsor chair, and took the chair opposite her, pushing it back a little out of range of the fire, which was clear and bright 'We didn't come just for tea,' he said.

'What then?' said Grandma, giving him a shrewd look.

'I've come to the conclusion that Tommy was innocent.'

'I'm not surprised. I thought you were working up to it.'

'It leads me to certain other conclusions, which I want to explain to Chris. I thought if you didn't mind listening—'

'Oh, I don't *mind*. Why should I? I expect if t' truth was known,' said Grandma with one of her grim smiles, 'I'm just as inquisitive as anybody else.'

'Then I'd better tell you what happened yesterday and today. Did Star tell you we'd gone to Carlington?'

'She did that.'

'Well, you see, it was like this ...' He made the story as brief as possible, but by the time it was finished the kettle had boiled and Chris had made the tea. 'How does that strike you, Grandma?' he said as he concluded.

She took her time to think about that. 'Wickedness,' she

said then. 'T' lad didn't have a chance, did he?'

'Is that how it strikes you? That he's more likely, rather than less, to be guilty of killing Neale.'

'I'm afraid so, Mr Maitland. There's that, and there's stealing. You don't look at it that way?'

'No, but I think I was half way convinced of his innocence before all this happened.' Grandma was struggling to her feet, and he waited until she had poured the tea and handed him his cup. Then he said slowly, 'That's not a feeling I can justify in any way at all. I can't give you a single reason, only I'm sure I'm right.'

'You were going to tell us your ideas,' said Chris. His mood seemed to have changed, or perhaps he just thought the other man was in need of encouragement.

'Yes, but they won't help at all,' said Antony. 'They're my ideas of what must follow if Tommy is *not* guilty. If anything, I think they'll make it more difficult for either of you to believe me.'

'Six impossible things before breakfast,' said Conway lightly. 'We both ought to be used to that by this time. You may as well go on.'

Grandma said nothing, just nodded at him when he looked at her enquiringly. Antony cleared his throat and said rather nervously, 'You did tell me Mrs Clayton's maiden name was Spencer, didn't you, Grandma.'

'I did.'

'Is she related in any way to Henry Spencer and Sons, lithographers and photo-engravers?'

'Henry Spencer is her brother.'

'Why on earth do you want to know that?' Chris demanded.

'I saw the obituary in the paper of a Joseph Taylor who had been in Spencers' employ.' Conway let that pass, though it wasn't really an answer at all, and Antony went straight on, as though somehow one thing led to another. 'If we

116

assume that Tommy did not rob the Claytons—'

'You've still got to explain why he went to the house,' said Chris.

'Yes, I know. I'll come to that in a moment. If we assume that, it becomes perfectly obvious that he was framed. And I see only one logical answer to the question. Who did the framing, or caused it to be done? Robert Clayton himself.'

Chris, in spite of his good resolutions, was moved to protest. 'No, look here, Antony. That's a bit thick.'

'I know it is. It has kept me in a state of dither for several days. All the same—'

'Robert Clayton is highly respected,' said Grandma in an expressionless voice.

'Yes, but he collects expensive things like Holbein miniatures. I don't know anything about the art world, but I should have thought they were only available to Galleries, or to millionaires. Even if his wife was wealthy in her own right ... have they any children?'

'Three. All in their teens,' Grandma told him.

'Another source of expense. You'll admit it's a possibility that he has another source of income.'

'Anything's possible, I suppose,' said Conway. But he did not sound convinced. Antony looked across at the old lady.

'What do you think about that?' he asked.

'It's possible, but is it likely?' she said roundly.

'That's the trouble. There are two possibilities, Tommy's guilt, or Clayton's. I've opted for the latter, but I can't give you any valid reasons for my choice.'

Old Mrs Duckett sipped her tea. 'Come now,' she said when she had put the cup down again, 'you must have some reason for believing in t' lad.'

'Well ... didn't he strike you as naturally truthful, Chris? And I can't see—I still can't see why he should have admitted breaking-in at the Claytons' and jibbed at admitting the rest of it, particularly when you explained to him that it might be a positive advantage to do so. He's an intelligent boy, you know, not dull.'

'Who knows what ideas a lad that age might get into his head?' said Chris slowly.

'I can see I'm not going to convince you. Will you at least listen to the rest of my story?'

Conway said, 'Of course.' Grandma nodded regally. Antony went on,

'I'm going out of chronological order again, but I think you'll see why in a minute. I think Tommy broke into the Claytons' house on Tuesday night, or early Wednesday morning, and was caught by the owner, who succeeded— where you and I failed for so long, Chris—in getting out of him what he was up to. He then imprisoned the boy, not in the house obviously, but somewhere, until the Friday morning when he released him, knowing he would go back to the hut and find Neale dead and the police in possession.'

'Wait a bit!' said Chris, interrupting. 'In your theory, did Mr Clayton kill the old man as well?'

'Yes. Killed him, or caused him to be killed.'

'You used that phrase before.'

'Because either is a possibility. I'm inclined to think that's the sort of job he wouldn't have entrusted to anybody else. And before you express your incredulity again, Chris, I have evidence for this, of a sort.'

'Let's hear it.'

'You admit the breaking-in. Tommy's fingerprints are proof enough of that. But why was he missing from his job with Curzon from the Wednesday onwards, and why did he turn up on Friday morning "looking like a little tramp" and hungry as well? Neale would never have tolerated the untidiness while Tommy was living with

118

him, you said yourself, Chris, he was a nut about clean-liness. Besides, if Tommy had hidden the miniatures him-self, in a bed that consisted of three mattresses piled together, he'd have damaged them seriously the first time he got into bed on top of them. And then there's the anonymous letter ... not nearly enough attention has been paid to that. It was written to get the police to the hut at a certain time, to coincide with Tommy's release, and that ties the murder and the burglary together ... don't you think?'

'I suppose it does fit together,' said Chris reluctantly. 'You're saying that Clayton hid the miniatures in the hut himself, to give Tommy a motive on the assumption that Neale had found them.'

'That's right. It does explain certain things that we were puzzled about, doesn't it?'

'Yes, but it's hard to believe ... why on earth should Mr Clayton do such a thing?'

Antony grimaced; the question had to be answered, but he knew that here he had not the faintest shred of evidence to offer. 'I have to admit that this part is mere guesswork,' he said, and hoped the admission would prove disarming. Chris ... he thought he had made some impression on Chris, but the old lady's face was expressionless and she had been silent now for too long altogether. 'It ties in—it might tie in with the reason Tommy had for attempting burglary. Suppose that Robert Clayton's second income comes from forgery, a highly organised business, exporting —say—$20.00 bills to America.'

'I suppose you've grounds for saying that somebody in this country is doing that.'

'I heard quite by chance ... something Chief Inspector Sykes told Jenny.'

'And you're building all this on the fact that Mr Clayton's brother-in-law is a lithographer?' Chris sounded doubtful, but at least he was considering the matter. 'Isn't that rather a shaky foundation?'

'There are two other ... straws in the wind, I suppose you might call them. One of Henry Spencer's employees died recently, I saw that in the paper. And Alfred Neale as a boy had considerable gifts as an artist; you told me that, Grandma.'

The old lady stirred in her chair as though she was growing restless. 'Aye, that I did,' she said heavily.

'You see what I mean now, don't you?'

'Let's see if I do.' Chris ticked the points off on his fingers. 'You're guessing—'

'I don't believe you like that word any more than Uncle Nick does,' said Antony sadly.

'I don't, but there's nothing else for it, is there? You're guessing that when Alfred Neale left Arkenshaw he earned his living as a photo-engraver, or something of the sort, and that part of his livelihood came from a dishonest use of his talents.'

'I'm guessing that,' said Antony, stressing the word. 'It would explain, wouldn't it, why religion hit him so hard when it did hit him? He was atoning for his past sins.'

'Yes, well, I'll grant you that. I suppose the next point is that Spencer's deceased employee was also a photo-engraver, dishonestly employed ... no, it still doesn't make sense.'

'Carry the argument a bit farther. Say that Robert Clayton knew about Neale's past, had some evidence of it perhaps. That isn't unlikely if they were all in the same racket. So when they were short of an engraver he called upon Neale to go back to his old profession. Neale refused indignantly, and later dispatched Tommy to burgle the Clayton's house and retrieve the proof of his iniquity. Clayton, realising that Neale in his new-found righteousness is a menace, murders him and frames Tommy. *Voila tout!*'

'But ... heavens above, Antony, if all that is true, why the devil didn't Tommy tell us about it?'

'We'll have no bad language in this house, Chris Conway,' said Grandma, enraged. 'Nor foreign talk either,' she added, with a baleful look in Maitland's direction. But for once in her life her admonitions fell upon stony ground, they were both too taken up with their argument to hear her.

'You'll grant me one thing, Chris,' Antony was saying, 'If we can get Tommy to talk, and if he corroborates what I'm telling you—'

'That would be different, of course.'

'Well, here I think I can convince you, even without that. You remember telling me during our first conversation about the case that the main thing that seemed to upset Tommy was seeing the psychiatrists?'

'Yes, I remember that.'

'And do you remember also how you induced him to talk to us at last about what happened in Carlington?'

'No, I ... what did I say?'

'I think I can quote your words exactly. You said, "With the best will in the world the jury will be swayed by what they hear in court. They'll be ready to think you're mad—" Do you remember saying that?'

'I may well have done, but—'

'And *then* he talked. He's frightened of going to prison, but he's far more frightened of being put in an asylum. Somebody's been deliberately scaring him ... don't you think?'

'But he might even be better off—'

'We know that, he doesn't. If a clever man, as Robert Clayton must be to have got where he is, set out to put the wind up him, don't you think he'd be able to do it? I think so, and I think he did it, and I'm not sure that isn't a worse sin than any other he's committed.'

There was a silence. Then Chris said tentatively, 'I'm bound to admit—' and broke off again when he heard old Mrs Duckett clear her throat ominously.

Antony turned to her, eager enough to substitute humour for emotion. 'Scurrilous talk, Grandma. I'm sorry. And I can't prove it either.'

'We'll say no more about that, Mr Maitland,' she told him graciously. 'If all this is true—'

'You're not saying you believe me!'

'It sounds to me a very reasonable story,' said Grandma surprisingly. 'And I can tell you two things that may help you. Winnie Spencer was supposed to be an heiress, but I can see now you're right about her not having t' kind of money to buy those miniatures. If they started off extravagant, 'appen it'd soon be used up. But Henry Spencer now, he inherited money too, and he went down south and put it in a publishing business and went bankrupt, so we heard. He came back to Arkenshaw ten years ago, and this Joseph Taylor who's just died about the same time. I've always supposed Robert Clayton helped his brother-in-law to get started in a new business, but I have been surprised once or twice at how well he seemed to be doing.'

'You mean, like Clayton, he spends more money than you think he should have.'

'He's a racing man, Mr Maitland ... well, that takes money, doesn't it? And he owns a horse or two, has them stabled over in York somewhere.'

'You're right, that does take money. What was your other point, Grandma?'

'I can tell you where they might have had t' lad hidden.'

'Can you though? Where?'

'Not so fast, Mr Maitland,' she rebuked his impatience. 'You'll know, Chris, that when Fred isn't on duty he takes me for a drive on Sunday afternoons. And if it isn't a very nice day sometimes we just drive around t' town, and see what's being built and what's being pulled down, and how places that we know are changing. So one day last month we went along Brinkley Drive.'

'You mean, you passed the Claytons' house? But they couldn't—'

'Just you let me tell this in my own way,' said Grandma, but now she sounded more indulgent than admonitory. 'There's t' garage, a bit away from t' house. A bit away from any other house, too. And there's a flat over, where t' chauffeur-handyman used to live, but this time all the windows were boarded up. So I asked Fred about it and he said t' last man had left, and when some vandals broke t' windows Mr Clayton had them boarded up, and that's how they'd stay until he got someone else to do t' job, and opened t' flat up again. If Tommy was hidden there nobody could see him, and nobody'd hear him either, even if he shouted and banged on t' door.'

'What if Mrs Clayton came to get her car? We've got to assume she isn't in the plot.'

'She doesn't drive.'

'How on earth do you know that, Grandma?'

'The housekeeper told Minnie Godfrey, and Minnie told me. Not that I encourage gossip, but that seemed harmless enough. It's along of having a chauffeur, I expect; when Mr Clayton's safely at the hospital, he's free to run her about. And just to round things off like, none of the children is old enough to drive.'

Antony was on his feet. 'Grandma,' he said, as he had once said to her years before, 'you're a jewel!' He ignored what could only be a cautionary sniff and whirled round on Chris. 'What,' he asked, 'do you think of *that*, my lad?'

Conway gave him a worried smile. 'Even before I heard what Grandma had to say I was going to admit you'd made out a good case. But I'm bound to add, Antony, that's because I know you. No-one else would believe it for an instant.'

'I know that.' His excitement died as quickly as it had arisen. 'I don't know what you think about it, Chris, but I think Tommy's going to have to tell this tale in court.'

'If he's as scared of what Clayton told him as you say he is—'

'Now that we know what's wrong, surely we can get round that? The thing that really worries me is that we'll be throwing him to the wolves in a way, in the person of Anderson, you know.

'Surely he wouldn't bully t' lad,' said Grandma, shocked.

'He'd ask him questions till he was dizzy, if that's any better. And the judge will protect Tommy, but only up to a point. Anderson looks on me as an adversary, you know, as someone trying to cheat him by any means at all, not as someone just trying to get at the truth. Tommy's story, if we can induce him to tell it, will be like a red rag to a bull.'

'But still you think that's the line we ought to work on,' said Chris, worried now.

'I'm afraid I do. We want to see Tommy now, and Bushey later this evening. Will you go and telephone, Chris, and see what you can arrange?'

When Conway had left the warm kitchen for the unwelcoming chill of Inspector Duckett's study, Maitland turned to old Mrs Duckett again. 'You've been more help than you know, Grandma. You've given me an idea.'

'Another idea,' she grumbled, but her expression softened as she gave him her hand. 'Not but what I'm glad you're doing your best for t' lad,' she said.

IV

Tommy wasn't reading that evening when they reached the attic room at the Remand Home. He was seated at the table, gazing down despondently at the scattered pieces of a large jigsaw puzzle, but if he was trying to assemble them he hadn't made much progress, only one corner was completed. He got up with apparent eagerness when the two men went in, but then a certain wariness supervened and he greeted them quietly. The warder took himself off; Maitland and Conway made their way to chairs on either side of the gas-fire, and Tommy turned his chair to face them. He said, in a depressed tone, 'I suppose you found Will.'

'Did you expect us to?'

'Oh, yes. He came to see mother so often, and he could only come when the *Red Jacket* was in port.'

'Well, you're quite right, we did find him. And he admitted—fairly readily—what he had done.'

'Did he say anything about me?'

'He told us to tell you he'd see you in court.'

'He wasn't ... angry?'

'He wasn't exactly pleased with us,' said Antony carefully, thinking back now with some surprise on what had happened that morning. 'But he certainly wasn't angry with you, Tommy.'

'What will they do to him?'

'I think ... we both think that the fact he has confessed will be a big point in his favour.' Tommy himself had mentioned his mother's teasing, but he didn't feel he could go into that too. 'But now I want you to think about your own affairs, and answer some more questions for us.'

'I'm sorry, Mr Maitland, really I am. There's nothing more I can tell you.'

'Let's see if we can't change your mind about that.'

'No. No, I can't!' Immediately he was in a panic.

'Listen to me for a moment, Tommy. Somebody told you—didn't they?—that if you talked about what happened people would think you were mad and you'd be sent to an asylum for the criminally insane.'

Tommy's eyes had widened as he listened, and his breath was coming rather quickly. 'How did you ... how could you know that?'

'I guessed,' said Antony, with a wry look for the word. 'You were also given, I think, a rather horrifying account of what went on in places like that.'

'I don't see how you know,' said Tommy. His lack of knowledge seemed to fill him with a sort of despair.

'Am I right?'

'Yes, he said—' He broke off there, and seemed to be making a deliberate effort to speak calmly. 'He said I'd be shut up with people who were really mad, and there was no knowing *what* they'd do, and anyway I'd soon be mad myself, living among them, and then I'd never get out. And he said the warders were always chosen for their brutality in places like that, but it was really that I couldn't see ... not to be shut up for ever!'

'Yes, I see, Tommy.' The boy's voice had risen as he spoke, and now Maitland's sounded unnaturally quiet. 'Will you believe me when I tell you—and Mr Conway will confirm it, if you like—that that was ... all lies.'

The quiet tones had their effect. 'Was it?' said Tommy. 'Was it really?'

'A pack of lies from beginning to end.' He paused, choosing his words, and then went on. 'Whatever the outcome of the trial, even if the verdict goes against you, if you tell what you know they may think you're an imaginative liar,

126

but they won't think you're mad. And whatever arrangements were made for your detention they'd take account of your age, and they wouldn't last for ever.'

'But you don't think, really, that I can get off.'

'I can't promise anything, Tommy. I wish I could, but I can't. What I do promise is that, if you'll give us your confidence, we'll do our best—Mr Conway and I—to get you acquitted. That's all I can promise, and if it isn't good enough—'

'You're talking now ... I didn't realise it at first, but you're talking now as if you didn't believe I'd killed Mr Neale.'

'I don't.'

'And neither do I, Tommy,' said Chris into the silence that followed. Tommy glanced from one to the other of them with a suddenly radiant look.

'Then I can tell you ... it's an awfully queer story,' he said.

'We're prepared for that.'

'Mr Maitland has been doing some more guessing,' said Chris.

'You couldn't guess this. It's far too—far too unlikely,' said Tommy positively. 'But if you think ... I'm trusting you both,' he added, and Maitland felt a sudden pang, because if his idea wasn't as good as he thought it ... but there was no time to think of that now.

'Go on with your story,' he said.

'I don't know where to begin. I suppose it was the Monday of the week Mr Neale died. I'd finished my errands, and had my supper, and he always made me go to bed at nine o'clock. I had thought of getting a torch, to read under the bedclothes, but there were only schoolbooks, he never would bring me anything from the library, so it didn't seem worth while. Well that night, after I was in bed, but I wasn't asleep of course, someone came to the hut.'

'Did you get up to look round the curtain?'

'No, it sounded important right from the beginning, but I thought if Mr Neale minded my being there he'd stop the other man while he sent me out. But I listened; I couldn't help it actually, but I think anyway I'd have been too interested not to.'

'Did they know each other?'

'Not to begin with. The visitor said something like, "Have I the honour of addressing Mr Alfred Neale?" He had a sarcastic sort of way with him. And when Mr Neale said, "Yes", he went on, "My name is Robert Clayton. You may have heard of me", and that time Mr Neale said, "No".'

Chris muttered under his breath, 'It's unbelievable,' and Antony gave him an amused look. But Tommy was too caught up in his story now to take any notice.

'The other man said, "That doesn't matter. *I* know *you*, Mr Neale, and that's all that need concern us." And Mr Neale said, "What do you know of me?" His voice sounded hard and angry, sort of, and even if I hadn't been keeping quiet before I'd have done so from then on, and I thought I'd pretend afterwards I'd been asleep and not heard anything. But while I thought that the other man was answering, "I know that you lived in Fulham for many years, and that while you were there you had two sources of income. And a former colleague of yours, now deceased, gave me a memento of those days, a photograph. Do I interest you now?" I'm not quoting their exact words, I don't suppose, but that was the way he talked.'

'That's all we need. The sense of what was said.'

'All right then. Mr Neale said something like, "Those days are behind me", and the other man laughed and said he had a proposition to make, and he wanted Mr Neale's help with a little matter ... "a matter which a man of your skill would find very simple," he said. And he said that because Joe Taylor—I think that was the name—was dead there was a vacancy in his organisation. And Mr Neale said in a dreadful voice, "Forgery! An abomination before the Lord", and that was the first time I realised what they were talking about, and of course I couldn't believe it at first. Not Mr Neale!'

'Looked at in one way, it might explain the violence of his conversation,' Antony told him.

'Do you really think so? I was just flabbergasted. They argued back and forth a good deal after that, and Mr Neale got very dramatic and biblical, and finally the other man said he hadn't really any choice, because the police would be interested in the photograph, "taken at number 23 Beale Street, in Fulham. You were a good deal younger then", he said, "but they couldn't fail to recognise you." But Mr Neale said, "No", and went on saying it, and at last the other man said he'd give him three days to think it over and then the photograph would go to the police, "anonymously", he said. And he gave his address, number 27 Brinkley Drive. And then he went away.'

'I expect,' said Chris, 'that he'd been quite sure to begin with that his proposition would be accepted. It would be only afterwards that he realised he'd have to silence Neale.'

Antony smiled at him, because Chris, once converted to an idea, was such an enthusiastic convert. 'You're getting ahead of the story,' he said. 'Let Tommy finish now.'

'There isn't much more,' Tommy assured him. 'I think Mr Neale must have forgotten all about me; I heard him walking about and muttering to himself for quite a long while, and when he came into the bedroom at last I pretended to be fast asleep and I think he must have believed me because he didn't say anything, then or the next day, about what had happened. But of course I couldn't help thinking about it, and I lay awake for ages that night wondering what to do. You see, I knew where

Brinkley Drive was, I'd been there with deliveries, and after all Mr Neale had been kind to me in his own way and I didn't want him to be sent to prison. And I knew he'd never give way and do what the man wanted, so I thought if I could find the photograph and get it back it would save a lot of difficulty. Of course, I didn't like the idea of breaking into somebody's house, I might not be able to find the photograph, and I was scared of being caught; but that was rather a cowardly attitude, so I decided to ignore it.

'Next night I waited until I was quite sure Mr Neale was asleep and crept out of the hut. It wasn't pay day, but there's one lady always tipped me when I took her order so I'd bought myself a flashlight, one of those small, flat ones that hardly showed in my pocket. It's quite a long way from the Town Allotments to Brinkley Drive, and the town was quiet, but I don't mind being out alone at night, I'm quite used to it. When I got there the house was quite dark, upstairs and down. I had my pocket knife, and there was a window that was like two doors at the side of the house, it was quite easy to open the latch. But I must have made more noise about it than I realised, because I'd hardly been inside a minute and was looking through the contents of a little desk that was in the room when the light came on and a big man came in. I tried to run away, but he grabbed me by the arm and made me sit down and started asking questions, and as soon as he spoke I knew he was the man who had been to see Mr Neale the night before. He asked me what I was doing there, and I felt I owed him an explanation, sort of, and besides if he knew I knew he was a forger he might not send for the police. But he wouldn't leave it there, he was very persistent and he hadn't known I was with Mr Neale, you see, so he wanted to know about that. And finally I told him everything, who I was and what had happened at home, but I didn't tell him about Will Roper. So then he said he was going to lock me up until he thought what to do with me, and he wouldn't listen when I asked him not to do that. And he told me to keep quiet because he said if anyone else heard us it would mean the police right away. And he made me go out with him the way I'd come, and along a path through the bushes until we came to the garage with windows above that were all boarded up. Inside was a kind of flat, quite comfortable but all dusty, as though there hadn't been anybody there for a long time. And that's where he left me, he said it was no use shouting because no-one would hear me, and if they did it wouldn't help me because then I'd go to prison. And the garage was so far from the house that I thought he was probably telling the truth about that, and I heard him take out his car in the morning, at least I suppose it was him, but nobody else came near the place all day.'

'Didn't he think to feed you?'

'Yes, when he came home next evening he brought me some sausage rolls and cornish pasties, and I could make tea in the kitchen so it wasn't too bad. But when I asked him what he meant to do with me he only smiled in a sinister sort of way and said I'd know in good time. And it was a whole day before I saw him again, the next evening I expected him about the same time but he didn't come until long after it was dark. I forgot to tell you he'd turned off the lights at the main switch, which must have been in the garage, but the boarding up hadn't been done very well at the kitchen window, so I could see a bit in there but nowhere else. Well, I heard the car and then the light in the sitting-room came on suddenly so I knew he must be on his way up and I got up off the bed and went in there to wait for him. And when he came in he was carrying Mr Neale's stick, and he didn't say a word, just came at me across the room as if he meant to get shot of me for good an' all,' said Tommy, reliving the moment, and departing for an instant from the high standard he had set himself, 'and I was that dazed, thinking he was going to hit me and I put out my hands and grabbed the stick as it came down. And then we stood there looking at each other, and he didn't try to get the stick away from me, just said very coldly, "I think if I were you I should let go of that, Tommy," and somehow I did as he said. And he went away without another word, but he turned the light out as he went. I couldn't understand what was happening at all, but I thought he must have been complaining to Mr Neale about me, and perhaps Mr Neale had lent him the stick, but then why hadn't he used it? It wasn't until you told me what the police said had happened when Mr Neale was killed that I saw that he'd deliberately framed me, and then I remembered that Mr Clayton had had gloves on.'

'But you didn't at that time feel you could tell us about it.'

'No, because of what he told me the next morning. He came upstairs when he came to get his car out and said I could go; but he told me all that you said about people believing I was mad if I said a word about what had happened, and he sounded awfully much as if he knew what he was talking about, so I was scared all over again. Then he went down and started his car and drove away, and I followed and went back to the hut because there didn't seem to be anywhere else to go. And, of course, Mr Neale was dead and that Superintendent Morrison was there.'

'Thank you, Tommy. That's all we need to know.'

'You do believe me, don't you?' He looked anxiously from one to the other of the two men. 'I know it doesn't really sound true,' he said.

'Well, you see, I'd worked some of it out for myself already,' said Maitland, almost as though he were apologising for some lapse of taste. 'Now, Tommy, the thing is, if we're to help you, you've got to help us. Will you be ready to repeat all that in court if it becomes necessary?'

'Will *he* be there?'

'Very probably, as he's already given his evidence. Of course, as a doctor he may ask permission to go about his own affairs, but I rather doubt it considering his interest in what's happening.'

'Well, all right, Mr Maitland. I'm trusting you,' said Tommy again. They spent nearly another hour going over and over the story, but that was what stuck in Antony's mind as they left.

As he started the car Chris said, looking straight ahead of him down the road, anywhere but at his companion, 'I suppose you realise that if things don't turn out as we hope—'

'Tommy will go to prison. Isn't that quite damnably enough.'

'More than enough. But it wasn't what I was going to say. Your reputation, after attacking a man of Mr Clayton's standing—'

'What about your own?' said Maitland, this time with half a smile. 'You're my instructing solicitor, after all.'

'Yes, but you're the one who will get the blame,' said Conway. He didn't sound happy about the idea.

'That's as it should be ... don't you think? I've already got a reputation for being unorthodox.'

'This is different.'

'Perhaps it is. I'm sorry, Chris, to be leading you into such a maze,' he added, and now he sounded wholly serious, 'but in the circumstances I can't think of anything else to do.'

V

That night he had more to tell Jenny, and even more
that couldn't be told just yet, not if he didn't want to
receive Sir Nicholas's curse by return of post. Jenny, as he
knew from experience wasn't very good at standing up
under cross-examination. So he told her that they now
knew who Tommy was and what had happened in Carlington on a night in early June and again that day; but he
didn't say a word about Tommy's later story or the decision
to which it had led him. But when he had finished his
narrative and was about to ring off she stopped him, saying,

'You're worried about something, Antony. What is it?'

'How do you make that out, love?'

'You haven't even mentioned the bedroom wallpaper.'

'No, I . . . well, I suppose as I haven't been inconvenienced
by it after all I haven't a right to grumble really.'

'You haven't told me—'

'Isn't this case enough to worry anybody? I'm worried,
Chris is worried, I daresay even Bushey is worried if the
truth were known.'

'You said if you once knew what Tommy was hiding
you'd see your way clear.'

'I may have said so, Jenny. If I did I was being absurdly
optimistic.'

'I thought perhaps he'd told you more than you said.'

'It's too late in the evening for mind-reading, love. What
you don't know won't hurt you.'

'I suppose that means there's something you don't want
Uncle Nick to know,' said Jenny, sad but resigned. 'All
right, Antony, I won't ask questions, but I do wish you'd
take care.'

'It's nothing like that,' said Antony hastily, and not altogether happily. 'Just a court manoeuvre he won't approve of, he'll hear of it soon enough.'

They rang off after that, and he went to bed wondering how far that last statement was likely to prove true.

I

When the court reconvened the next morning it might
have been observed by anybody watching with close
attention that some disagreement seemed to have arisen
in the ranks of the defence. Maitland and Bushey were
arguing hotly, and once when Conway ventured to put in
some remark on one side or the other Maitland turned on
him almost viciously. The entrance of the judge put an
end to these antics, of course, but even then there were
some resentful glances passed between them. After a while
Conway tapped Maitland's shoulder, and when he turned
round handed him a scribbled note. Antony took it eagerly,
but it said only, 'Clayton's here!'

As Maitland had foreseen, Superintendent Morrison's
evidence was gone into again at length; certainly Anderson
was leaving no chance that the jury wouldn't have it well
in mind when they came to consider their verdict. Maitland
himself had a few questions, after the direct examination
was finished.

'I am interested in the anonymous letter, Superintendent.
We have all seen the letter, the rough printing on cheap
paper, the postmark ARKENSHAW 8 P.M. You say, too,
that there were no fingerprints on the letter itself ...
somebody then had been very careful. What I want to
know is, can you explain this letter in any way?'

'Somebody wanted us to know where the miniatures
were hidden.'

'Yes, Superintendent, that is obvious. Now let us take
it a step farther. On the assumption that Tommy was the

thief, can you hazard a guess as to who the writer of the letter might have been?'

Morrison took his time to think about that. 'No, I can make no such guess,' he said at last.

'Inexplicable,' said Maitland, dismissing the matter, and turning to the next subject before Anderson could object. 'Didn't it surprise you to find the door of the hut ajar?'

'No. No, I don't think it did particularly.'

'That is something else I should like to have explained.'

'I think the accused left it open himself.'

'When he ran away after killing Alfred Neale?' said counsel, with an inflection of sarcasm in his voice.

'That's what I think,' said Morrison stolidly.

Antony, as he prepared his next question, was conscious of a warm feeling of liking for the man. He was doing his job as well as he could, but there wasn't an ounce of animus in him. 'Horrified by what he had done, no doubt.' Maitland's tone was still scornful. 'Why then, if we assume his guilt—as you are doing, I think, Superintendent—why then did he come back?'

'I think that if he intended to run away again he may have needed money. There was money in the hut, as I have told the court.'

'Appalled at one moment, coolly calculating the next. That would be a strange mixture even if we were talking of a grown man. Tommy, I would remind you is thirteen years old.'

'I am in no danger of forgetting that.'

'Very well then. What was his demeanour when he came into the hut and found you there?'

'He looked scared.'

'Did he look as if he expected to find Neale dead?'

'I can't answer that question. When I turned and saw the boy he must already have seen Neale's body.'

'So there is nothing inconsistent with his being surprised as well as frightened.'

'Nothing inconsistent, no.'

'What was the condition of the hut when you examined
it?'

'Apart from Neale's body it was extremely clean and
orderly.'

'And how did Tommy look when you first saw him?
Physically, I mean, not his expression.'

'Grubby and untidy.'

'I see. That's interesting, isn't it?'

'I'm afraid I don't follow you.'

Something in Maitland's tone had put Anderson on the
alert. The judge looked up too, frowning. 'Did he look like
a boy who had been living in that clean and orderly hut
with an old man who had something of an obsession on
the subject of cleanliness?' said Maitland, and swept on
without giving the witness time to reply. 'Did he not rather
look like a boy who had been shut up somewhere for three
days, with no-one to see that he washed his hands before
meals and didn't sleep in his clothes?'

The judge said, 'Mr Maitland!' protestingly, and Maitland, who had seated himself again, looked up and smiled
at him. Anderson half rose to his feet, and then subsided.
The witness said, 'Well, I suppose—' weakly, and allowed
the sentence to trail into silence when he saw that counsel
had already forgotten him. And John Bushey shrugged
his shoulders and turned and said something angrily to
Chris Conway, sitting behind him. There was a brief, but
significant silence, before Mr Justice Gilmour said pettishly,
'Do you wish to re-examine the witness, Mr Anderson?'

'No, my lord. If my learned friend has no further
questions,'—Maitland shook his head—'you may stand
down, Superintendent, thank you,' said Anderson. For
some reason he couldn't explain he felt uneasy.

One change had been made in Maitland's projected plan of action, at the prosecution's request. ('Falling over themselves to be fair,' he had commented cynically to Chris when he heard of it.) Both the Detective Inspector from Carlington, who could give evidence as to Tommy's identity, and William Roper were to be called as prosecution witnesses. The first appeared before the court adjourned for luncheon, and caused something of a sensation, though he told his story in the most matter-of-fact of tones; the second gave evidence after the recess and caused a temporary uproar, to the great distress of the judge, whose worst fears were all being confirmed.

Of the Detective Inspector Maitland had only one question, or a series of questions, to ask. 'Was Tommy Ridehalgh known to you prior to his mother's death?'

'I knew of him,' said the witness cautiously.

'As a boy whose home life was such that he spent a great deal of time roaming the streets, especially late at night?'

'I was aware of that fact.'

'But you never knew him in your professional capacity, so to speak? He was never in any trouble?'

'Never,' said the witness, commendably brief.

That was before lunch.

Immediately after the recess there was another surprise, no less sensational in its way. John Bushey reappeared in court only to ask, and receive the judge's permission to retire from the case, 'because of differences with my learned friend, Mr Maitland, as to its conduct.' Mr Justice Gilmour inclined his head graciously, but his tone was decidedly querulous when he asked, 'Are you prepared to proceed alone, Mr Maitland?'

'Quite prepared, my lord,' said Maitland readily. In some odd way, Bushey's defection seemed to have raised his spirits. He smiled at the judge again, and Gilmour said,

'Hmph,' in a decidedly grumpy tone.

Will Roper's evidence-in-chief was kept to the bare bones of his statement, no defence or explanation of his conduct asked or offered. He sounded stiff and ill-at-ease, and—in spite of the message he had sent the boy—he did not look at Tommy. When the usher's bellows for 'Silence!' had finally been obeyed, and the pandemonium had died down again, Anderson had already seated himself and Maitland was on his feet, waiting to cross-examine.

'Mr Roper, I wonder if you would mind telling us why you came here today.'

Will looked for the moment completely distraught. 'Why ... you know—'

'Tell the court, Mr Roper.'

'Because ... well, because of Tommy. In case anyone thought he'd done her in.'

'Who had done what?' said the judge.

'I understand Mr Roper to mean, your lordship, that in view of the charge already laid against Tommy—that of murdering Alfred Neale—he felt there was some danger of his being accused also of his mother's murder,' said Maitland glibly.

Gilmour looked suspiciously from him to the witness and back again, said 'Thank you,' dubiously, and waved a hand as a signal to proceed.

'You know Tommy quite well, don't you?'

'Yes, I do.'

'And have a regard for him.'

'I always liked the lad.'

'Still, I am probably right in saying—am I not?—that you would not have come forward today, and incriminated yourself as you have, if you had thought there was the faintest chance that he is guilty as charged.'

'If you mean, did he kill the old man there's all the fuss about, of course he didn't! A lot of nonsense, that is.'

'Thank you, Mr Roper, that is all.' All he could hope for, and perhaps more than he had expected. But he didn't deceive himself that the overall picture had been changed. Once he had made his own opening statement he was committed to putting Tommy into the witness box tomorrow, with results that might well be disastrous for both of them. Unless ... unless—

He wondered suddenly, irrelevantly, what use John Bushey was making of his unexpectedly free afternoon.

That concluded the case for the prosecution. It was still only a little past three o'clock when Maitland got up to make his opening speech for the defence. He realised as he did so that he was nervous, and that it would be fatal to let his nervousness show. (There they were, all twelve of them, and not a clue to what they were thinking. Probably that it was chilly in the courtroom, and it would be nice to get out into the sunshine and go home to tea.) '—I am sure my learned friends for the prosecution will agree with me that this is a particularly distressing case, in that the whole panoply of the law is arrayed against a boy only thirteen years old. In other circumstances I might make much of my client's youth, stressing how difficult it is to envisage a boy his age having the good taste to select the Holbein miniatures out of the many beautiful and valuable articles which no doubt enrich Mr Robert Clayton's collection.' (That was a good line, better stick with it for a moment or two.) 'He could hardly have been conscious of their value; and if by some freak he had been aware of it, where did he intend to dispose of them? From what we have been told of Alfred Neale a more unlikely candidate for the position of partner in crime does not exist. But if this picture attracts you, if you feel that perhaps Neale was not so white as he has been painted, where then is the prosecution's case? They rely, as my learned friend has explained to you, on the premise that Alfred Neale was outraged and horrified when he discovered the theft. So he would have been, so I am sure he would have been, but I shall hope to show you, by my client's testimony, that the theft never took place.' (That ought to hold them for a while, the first hint they've had that the defence don't mean to rely on a plea of something like self-defence. And it ought to shake that bastard Clayton too; he'll know now that Tommy has talked to me.)

'There has been a good deal of talk and conjecture over the fact that my client, Tommy Ridehalgh, refused until this last weekend to give his name in full, or to state where he came from. This weekend the mystery of his identity was solved by the police, and when I talked to him he was able to tell me, as he will tell you himself from the witness box, the reason for his silence. As Mr Roper, whose evidence you have just heard, has a regard for Tommy, so that he would not willingly involve him in his crime, so Tommy also had a regard for Mr Roper, that made him run away from his home rather than give evidence that would condemn his friend. This is why I can say to you, and say it with confidence, that he would never have turned, whatever the provocation, on the old man who had befriended him.

'Let me tell you a little about Tommy's background ...' That was safe enough, stick with it for a while. The thing was to spin it out, so that by the time he had finished the judge would be ready to adjourn, and Tommy would not be called until tomorrow. And he must say enough to alert Clayton, but not enough to give the game away altogether. One word too much and the thing was hopeless. He made a conscious effort to rid himself of all outside influences, to concentrate on spinning words ...

The judge thought it was a pity Maitland was throwing away what might have been a good defence. It wouldn't have secured the release of the prisoner, of course, but a boy like that should be somewhere he could be taken care of, by people who knew how to handle him, not at large where he might someday be subject to another murderous rage. Maitland had a name, of course, for pulling off a tricky defence, but this time, Mr Justice Gilmour considered, he wouldn't be so lucky. He hadn't forgiven counsel yet for the shameless display of fireworks earlier in the day. Of course, nothing had been said to connect Maitland with the appearance of William Roper, and he—the judge—had no quarrel with that, no quarrel at all, but the affair had been managed in such a way as to encourage cheap sensationalism. Unconventional, to say the least. And everybody knew Maitland had a reputation for the unconventional.

William Anderson Q.C. was quite simply angry. There was only one honest way of dealing with the defence, and anybody else would have taken it. He did not stop to consider that he would have been just as resentful whatever Maitland had done; the only consolation was that his learned friend seemed to be in a fair way to making a fool of himself, and that was something he would like to see. All this talk of what the boy's story would be, he discounted that. Something Maitland had put him up to, most likely. Well, he would have something to say about that himself when the time came. A difficult business, of course, cross-examining a boy that age without seeming to press him, but he thought he could trust himself to do it fairly enough when the time came.

Chris Conway listened unhappily to Maitland's speech, and thought it was all very clever, very specious, but by itself, or even backed up by Tommy's story tomorrow, it wouldn't convince anybody at all. He had to exert a considerable effort of will to keep himself from glancing in Robert Clayton's direction. By this time he must guess what was up, and either the bait had been taken or it hadn't. If not, if the surgeon had the sense to let things ride, tomorrow would be a nasty anticlimax; and what would be said about Maitland, trying without a shred of evidence to blacken an innocent man's name, didn't bear thinking of. That his own reputation might suffer equally he was inclined to doubt, having very little improper pride, and feeling himself in this to be in an altogether subordinate position. Even Maitland's anxious, 'I won't drag you into this against your will,' the night before had made very little impression on him. So now he listened, and admired, and looked very nearly as worried as he was. And Maitland went on talking.

Over at the side of the courtroom, where the witnesses who had already given evidence were seated, Robert Clayton listened impassively. Even if Chris had been betrayed into the indiscretion of glancing his way there would have been nothing to tell what he thought of the performance.

When the courtroom clock showed the hour to be nearing half past four, Maitland judged it safe to have done. The judge would never submit a boy of Tommy's age to the ordeal of giving evidence at the end of a long and tiring day. '... and on all these matters,' he said, and for all anybody could tell at that point he might have been prepared to speak all night, 'Tommy Ridehalgh will speak for himself. He will answer the questions which for so long he was unwilling to answer, even to his lawyers; and he will explain the reason, with which you will all sympathise, for his reticence. I shall not ask for any special consideration for his youth, his story will speak for itself, and when you have heard it you will be convinced, as I am, that he is innocent not only of murder, but of the theft of which he is accused.' He bowed to the judge, turned a little to bow also to the jury, and sat down with a swirl of his gown. Conway said in his ear, 'A marathon performance,' and he looked round and said in a tight voice,

144

'For good or ill, Chris. For good or ill. Wouldn't you like to know what the harvest will be?'

The judge had gone. There was a general move to leave the courtroom. Robert Clayton got up and stretched and said to his neighbour on the right as they moved towards the door. 'Most impressive indeed. An almost perfect example of how to make bricks without straw.'

II

The newspapers that evening were full of all the kinds of things that Sir Nicholas deplored, and it was a pretty safe bet, Antony considered, that the London papers would have the same story tomorrow morning, in even greater detail. As if that weren't bad enough, he had to endure some quite efficient cross-examination from his colleagues in the Bar Mess, when he joined them in time for a drink before dinner. As far as Will Roper's unexpected appearance was concerned, they had unerringly cast him for the role of *deus ex machina*, and nothing he could say would convince them to the contrary. By the time they sat down to table things had quietened down somewhat, but Maitland's nerves were too raw that evening for him to appreciate the good-natured interest his affairs had aroused. Only Anderson took no part in the banter, he had that evening what Antony described to himself as a look of secret satisfaction, which boded ill for the morrow.

But at last the evening was over. They parted noisily in the hall, drifted in ones and twos up the staircase. Antony went along with the rest of them, turned left when he reached the first floor, said 'Good-night,' to a man called Preston half way along, and then continued to his own room at the end of the corridor. He stood a moment with his hand on the knob, his ears alert for every sound, then with sudden decision turned the key, flung the door open and went in. He still stood indecisively for a second or two, and then shrugged and moved across to the dressing-table, removing his tie as he went.

A moment later there came a tapping, low but insistent, upon the door.

Again there was a second's hesitation before he called, 'Come in,' but when there was no response he went across the room quickly and pulled the door open with an impatient gesture. 'What the—?' he started. And then, in a stupefied tone, 'Mr Clayton!' (Now, did that sound genuinely surprised, or didn't it?)

Evidently it did. Robert Clayton smiled and came forward with a gently crowding movement, so that Maitland gave way, step by step, in front of him. 'You didn't expect to see me here,' Clayton said, with satisfaction.

'No, and I . . . I don't know what you're doing here, but I can't talk to you. A prosecution witness—'

'Ah, yes. Professional etiquette forbids it, does it not? If it will make things any easier for you I think I can promise not to mention my own evidence at all. Meanwhile—' he turned as he spoke, turned the key in the lock and shot the safety catch '—we may as well be private.'

Antony had backed as far as the window by now. 'I think you're mad,' he said, but he sounded nervous and uncertain, and the other man laughed.

'When you put on that—would it be unkind to call it a performance?—in court today,' he said, 'I really think you should have foreseen some such outcome as this.'

'What do you want?'

'Why, to talk to you, of course. To save you, if possible, from making an abject fool of yourself tomorrow. But aren't you going to ask me to sit down?'

'It hadn't occurred to me.'

'No, it is I who want this conference. I suppose it is no

146

use telling you that it is in your own interests to listen to me.' He sighed as Antony shook his head. 'You must give me credit for a little forethought, I came prepared to enforce my wishes if necessary,' he said, pushed back his raincoat to come at his jacket pocket the more easily, and pulled out a large, old-fashioned looking pistol, looking from it to Maitland with an almost sheepish air. 'You must forgive the melodrama, it isn't at all the sort of thing I go in for, but in the circumstances you leave me no alternative.'

'You *are* mad,' said Maitland with conviction.

'I shall hope to convince you otherwise.' He was crossing the room as he spoke, keeping well clear of the window, until he came to the bench in front of the dressing table. He sat down on it, facing Antony, and with the skirts of his raincoat spread out behind him. 'I shall make myself comfortable, if you will not,' he said. 'It is interesting to meet you out of court like this, Mr Maitland. The wig makes a difference, but I think I should have known you, even if I hadn't expected to find you in this room.' He looked quite at his ease, the gun held slackly on his knee, but there was menace in every inch of him and somewhere in Maitland's mind a small, self-mocking thought struggled for recognition. He had got what he had been playing for, all that long afternoon in court, and now how little he liked it.

'It occurs to me,' he said, with what sounded like an unconvincing attempt at bravado, 'that standing here I present rather too good a target.' He took a step sideways, to the room's one armchair, turned it a little to face Clayton more directly, and sat.

'That's better!' said Robert Clayton, with some satisfaction evident in his voice. 'Now we can talk like sensible men. But first I must ask you—I'm really interested to know the answer—what on earth made you think you could get away with that story of Tommy's. You can't possibly have any evidence to back it up.'

'I happen to believe him,' said Maitland quietly.

'That isn't the point, though I suppose I should congratulate you on persuading him to give you his confidence. But as for calling him as a witness, you should know better, a man of your experience.'

'Perhaps I also believe the truth should be told,' said Maitland, his mouth wry.

'Regardless of consequences? My dear fellow!'

'Wait a bit! How do you know what Tommy told me?' said Antony, and held his breath for the reply.

'I presume,' said Clayton carelessly, 'that he told you the truth.'

If Antony felt a sudden stab of exultation, his face did not show it. He said woodenly, 'His story had gaps, inevitably. But the implication was that you killed Neale yourself.'

'It wasn't, you see, the kind of thing I should care to trust to a subordinate,' said Clayton, exactly as if he were apologising for the fact. 'But this is getting us nowhere. This quixotic scheme of yours—'

'I faced the consequences before ever I got up in court today.'

'Then I needn't enlarge on them. Tommy is telling lies, too complicated for him to have thought up for himself. That's what everyone will think. Who will get the credit for having coached him in them? You have a certain reputation, Mr Maitland, which won't help you at this point.' He saw Antony's lips tighten, and laughed again. 'Well, well, I see you've thought of all that for yourself. But will Tommy be one penny the better off for all this self-sacrifice? You know he won't.'

'Is that what you came here to say to me?'

'Not entirely. If you can't help Tommy, what is the

148

use of going on with this programme? I admit—I'm being perfectly honest with you—I admit it would embarrass me.'

'Surely not!' There was the bite of sarcasm there, and Clayton shot him a sudden, startled look. But his voice was as suave as ever as he went on.

'The police wouldn't believe it, too unlikely a tale. The general public would sympathise with me. But my associates, Mr Maitland, that's a different story. They trust my organising ability, and might feel that in this instance I have let them down. You can see that the situation is ... awkward.'

'Do you expect me to sympathise with you too?'

'I thought you might be brought to see my point of view. For a consideration, of course.'

'I ... see.'

'I don't think you do, quite. In return for your co-operation I am prepared to offer you almost any sum in cash that you care to name.'

'In counterfeit notes?' asked Maitland ironically.

'In perfectly genuine currency, my dear fellow. There's no difficulty about that.'

'No, I don't suppose there would be. But having gone so far—'

'I'm sure your ingenuity is equal to thinking up some tale to explain Tommy's failure to give evidence tomorrow. He'll do what you tell him, won't he? Fake a nervous breakdown, something like that. Then you can apologise to the court for the remarks you made during your opening address ... say you realise that Tommy's mental condition is such that after all no reliance can be placed on his word ... that kind of thing.'

'I can hardly ... this needs some thought.'

'Your own position would be better than if you went ahead as planned, even apart from the monetary angle.

Your junior disagrees with you so violently that he has already retired from the case. I don't imagine you'd have any difficulty with young Conway, do you?'

'Perhaps not.'

'His *penchant* for retaining your services has not gone unremarked in Arkenshaw, and I don't think anyone is in doubt which of you is the stronger character.' He waited a moment, but when Maitland did not speak went on in a rallying tone, 'Take your time over it, it's too good an offer to turn down. Meanwhile, you might tell me, what made you believe Tommy?'

'There were details in his story that rang true. I'd already worked out for myself that if he weren't guilty you must be, so I wasn't altogether unprepared for what he told me.' He spoke abstractedly, but then gave his head a shake as though to clear it. 'I admit I was held up for some time by the coincidence which made Tommy the logical suspect for not one, but two murders.'

'But, my dear Mr Maitland, it wasn't a coincidence! Tommy's story—I induced him to confide in me very fully, you know—gave me the idea of killing Neale in perfect safety and framing him for the murder. And at that time, of course, I thought he had killed his mother, so it seemed like poetic justice. You really can't call it a coincidence.'

'No, I see.' He thought for a moment and then said, rather abruptly, 'This offer of yours ... I'd like to know more about your organisation, you know.'

'If you're thinking we may be uncovered, set your mind at rest. Everything is most carefully worked out. There is my brother-in-law, my junior partner as you might say. That's how it has turned out over the years, though it was he who first interested me in the venture. It all arose from his meeting with Joe Taylor ... but you aren't interested in that. There is the man who works overtime to run the printing press, and two men—quite above suspicion, I assure you—who act as couriers in taking the currency abroad. Through them I have connections in London, and I hope that the task of replacing Joe Taylor will not be too difficult.'

'I'm surprised in that case that you tried to recruit Alfred Neale.'

'At the time it seemed logical enough. I was in a position to threaten him—'

'Yes, how did that come about? Tommy mentioned a photograph.'

'Neale had worked in his time in London for a similar organisation to my own. Taylor was employed by them at the same time. The snapshot was taken, I think, in a spirit of foolery, but its details were extraordinarily clear. It showed Neale, and it showed the tools of his trade. Nobody with the slightest knowledge of our line of work could have doubted for a moment what he had been doing.'

'I haven't "the slightest knowledge" I'm afraid.'

'The snapshot showed him touching up the enlarged negative of a bank note, but that's neither here nor there.'

'How did it come to be in your possession?'

'Through Taylor. He showed it to me when Neale first took possession of the nissen hut. He seemed amused by what he had heard of his having "got religion". So I asked if I might keep it, against a rainy day, you know. Does that answer all your questions?'

'I think so. At least, there's one more. What happens if I refuse this proposition of yours?'

'Now I hoped you wouldn't ask me that. Why think of anything so disagreeable?'

'If you mean you'd shoot me, I don't see how you could get away with it.'

'Nothing easier.'

'If Tommy talked—'

'I doubt if he would, with your influence removed. But

if he did, they'd still think it was your imagination that was behind it. And if anyone questioned my movements, which I doubt, I am at present playing chess with my brother-in-law. His family know better than to interrupt us for anything short of an earthquake, and it is quite customary for us to play into the small hours.'

'You've been waiting in the hotel until I came up to bed.'

'In the bathroom opposite, the one that serves the back rooms that don't have their own. I know this hotel rather well, you see. And I assure you I took care not to be seen coming in, which I didn't do by the main door, and I shall take equal care not to be seen leaving. I have explained why I should prefer not to have to take this drastic course of action, but I assure you I shall not hesitate if you force my hand.'

'You had to find out my room number.'

'A telephone call, what simpler? As for the reason for your murder, have your activities made no enemies for you through the years? I think the police will be very satisfied with that conclusion.'

'This conversation is beginning to depress me.'

'There is no reason for that, after all.'

'Not really. I take it you're not prepared to carry out your threat before witnesses.' He paused, watching while Clayton's manner changed from self-confidence to an uneasy doubt, and then said, very gently, 'This is one of the front rooms that have their own bathrooms, you know. And my friends have been waiting even longer than you have.'

Following his eyes, Clayton glanced quickly over his shoulder and saw Superintendent Morrison, closely followed by Inspector Thorpe and Chris Conway, coming into the room.

Nobody had ever called Robert Clayton a stupid man.

He refused to talk as stubbornly as ever Tommy Ridehalgh had done, but he made no difficulty about surrendering his gun and accompanying the police.

The new and even more astounding sensation didn't appear in the press until the evening papers were out, but they were already on the streets when Antony and Chris Conway called on old Mrs Duckett just about in time for tea. 'So you managed it after all, Mr Maitland,' said Grandma, when Chris had picked up the heavy iron kettle and gone into the scullery to fill it.

'It worked, Grandma. It might easily not have done,' said Antony. He sounded tired, and she gave him one of her sharp looks. 'Looking back on it now, the hardest part was persuading Superintendent Morrison to take part in such a very undignified charade, but he was worried enough by what I told him not to be able to square it with his conscience to ignore it altogether. And when he knew Bushey had agreed to take part in the proceedings by disowning me in open court ... he has a great regard for Bushey's common sense.'

'Aye, he's a good man, t' Superintendent.'

'It was nearly as bad getting him to let me attend as well,' said Chris, coming out of the scullery and setting the kettle down firmly on the bars of the range. 'And I wouldn't have missed it for a fortune.'

'I'm glad somebody enjoyed the entertainment,' said Antony dryly.

'You played up to him very well. You had him believing just what you wanted him to believe,' said Chris enthusiastically. Antony gave his head a sudden, decisive shake.

'He's been a power in this town too long, he's almost a

megalomaniac now, I think. He couldn't believe Alfred Neale would refuse to do what he wanted, which started all the trouble. He couldn't believe either that I wouldn't agree to his proposition; I hoped that's the way it would be, but I couldn't be sure.'

'I don't understand exactly what happened today,' said Grandma. 'Fred told me t' gossip at dinner time, but he didn't know any details.'

'Anderson indicated the Crown's intention not to proceed with the prosecution, which was formally entered on the record. That's just a quick way of doing things, to get Tommy free before they finished preparing their case against Clayton.'

'Isn't it enough evidence, what two policemen heard him say?'

'They'll want more than that for the trial, but I don't think Morrison is too worried about that. Once you know where to look—'

'So that's all right then, isn't it? What about young Tommy?'

'He's back at the Remand Home for the moment. I think there'll be some kind of a hassle as to whether they put him in an orphanage here or in Carlington.' He broke off, and gave her rather a one-sided smile. 'Not really a very happy ending, is it, Grandma?'

Chris, who had been making and pouring the tea, went back to his place with his cup. 'We've been thinking about that,' he said, stirring industriously. 'Star thought perhaps we might take him in, at least until after Robert Clayton's trial.'

'Star's too young to be dealing with a hulking lad of thirteen,' said Grandma roundly. 'Besides, she has enough to do with baby ... and probably more to come,' she added, directing a look at Chris that made him choke over his tea. 'Not but what I don't think an orphanage is at all a good idea, from what you've told me of t' lad.'

'That's what I think,' said Antony helplessly. 'But what *are* we to do?'

'Aye, I can see it's worrying you. You'll bring him to me, Mr Maitland,' said Grandma Duckett imperiously.

'So that's what we did,' he told Jenny, when he got back to Kempenfeldt Square the next afternoon. 'There were some formalities, of course, but on the whole I think the authorities were as relieved as I was.'

'Antony, did you deliberately—?'

'No, of course not. It never occurred to me.'

'Will it work, do you think?'

'Like a charm, love. At least Tommy will never be in any doubt again that somebody takes an interest in his doings.'

Jenny laughed. 'No, I can imagine that. But what about Inspector Duckett, didn't she even consult him?'

'Told him, more likely. But I saw him in the evening and all he said was, "I'm suited". And he and Grandma between them did a pretty good job of bringing up Star, didn't they? So I should think it will work out very well.'

'That's all right then. I ought to warn you, Antony, that Uncle Nick is coming to dinner tonight.'

'It's Wednesday!' said Maitland, outraged. 'He must have been here last night.'

'Yes, but he practically ordered me to ask him again this evening. It was dreadful, Antony,' she went on, with relish. 'He brought *all* the evening papers with him, and he told me exactly what he thought of you—'

'But nothing that happened was my fault!'

'You can try telling him that, of course, if you think it'll do any good,' said Jenny, laughing at him. 'But, darling, you haven't said once you're glad to be home.'

'I *was*. Yes, love, and I like the "unusual" paper in the bedroom, and the new paint in the bathroom, and I'll try not to scream when we get the bill, but tell me one thing before I die of suspense: did you remember to get another bottle of brandy?'

'When I knew Uncle Nick was in a mood, of course I did. Very special—'

'So I should hope.'

'No, I mean *extra* special. In all the circumstances.'

Antony leaned back and closed his eyes. 'How much?' he demanded faintly.